MW00465331

FLAME OF THE ROCKIES

QUEEN OF THE ROCKIES — BOOK 6

ANGELA BREIDENBACH

May God bless you!

Angie

Copyright © 2021 by Angela Breidenbach
Angela E. Breidenbach, LLC. All rights reserved.
No part of this book may be reproduced in any form or by any electronic or mechanical means, including information storage and retrieval systems, without written permission from the author, except for the use of brief quotations in a book review. Write for permission to Angela@angelabreidenbach.com.

ISBN 13 paperback: 978-1-957132-07-5
ISBN Ebook: 978-1-957132-09-9
ISBN Large Print: 978-1-957132-08-2
Fiction/Historical/Religious
Cover Design by Jenneth Dyck.

This book is a work of fiction set in a real location. Any reference to historical figures, locations, or events, whether fictional or actual, is a fictional representation. Originally published as Seven Medals and a Bride. Biblical verses in this book of fiction are taken from Holy Bible, King James Version, KJV, Cambridge, 1769.

Scripture quotations marked (NLT) are taken from the Holy Bible, New Living Translation, copyright © 1996, 2004, 2007 by Tyndale House Foundation. Used by permission of Tyndale House Publishers, Inc., Carol Stream, Illinois 60188. All rights reserved.

Published in Missoula, Montana, by Gems Books, an imprint of Gems of Wisdom/Angela E Breidenbach LLC.

Published in Missoula MT, USA

FLAME OF THE ROCKIES

ACKNOWLEDGMENTS

I'm grateful to my family for riding the Hiawatha three times with me for research and fun!

Thank you to those who have gone before, battled deprivation, tamed the wild that we may enjoy our lives today!

To all our heroes unknown, unsung
All the statues as yet undone
The Lord sees all and will not forget
Earthly sacrifice and commitment
—Angela Breidenbach

INTRODUCTION

On the border of the Idaho panhandle and the western edge of Montana you'll find the Route of the Hiawatha. Today, it's a magical bike trail through old train tunnels, across towering trestle tracks, and a slight slope most of the way down.

Stay tuned for the Montana Travel Tips article at the end of this story for the Hiawatha travel tips.

Taking the trail slow is the only way to see all the historic signs that inspired this story, Flame of the Rockies. The signs tell more than the history. The signs tell of a hardy people who dared to live in such a wilderness. A wilderness where civilization wandered along the rails scratching out fortunes and futures among over more than seventy-five ethnic groups.

There are stories of the elegant train tours, marked graves, abandoned shanty towns, mining operations, wild bars and bordellos, schools and chapels, and heroic efforts to save lives during The Big Blow Up.

The Big Blow Up is the largest fire in US history.

Over three million acres burned because of lightning strikes, winds, and sparks from the rails. I'm sure you've heard of the "perfect storm", this was the perfect fire storm. A storm that wiped out the world as we knew it. Entire forests of ancient trees gone, tiny towns razed, and mines devastated. A complete system of connected economic and relational people pushed out by nature's fury.

Into this setting, I put a romance between the fictional widow of a man who really existed and a hero who might have existed. I found the story between the lines on those historical signs I read on one of our many family rides down the Hiawatha. A story that wouldn't leave me alone building in adventure and the sheer will to survive that those historic markers convey. A story to remember what all those people went through en masse and how others put their own lives at risk to bring those they loved and those they didn't even know to safety.

If you'd like to read more about the Big Blowup, here's a really good article with a map that I enjoyed reading. But to experience the depth of the story, well, you'll have to take your own ride down the Hiawatha. But before you do, let me bring the whole thing to life for you complete with the true history of all the ethnic groups working in the mines and on the rails, women who baked bread and fed those men, and the towns that built up around the high-paying jobs the railroads and mining companies offered.

https://www.fs.usda.gov/Internet/ FSE_DOCUMENTS/stelprdb5444731.pdf

One of the most interesting elements to me was the

danger of rail and mine workers, though important, paled in the face of food quality. Hence, we meet our heroine, a bread baker. Men would hear of the higher quality food and higher wages at the Milwaukee Railroad. They'd come despite the danger for the opportunity to change the lives of their families, many brining families later or marrying from the bakers and bordello ladies. But it was the food the railroad company provided that became famous. Famous enough to siphon men from other projects all around the world. A man who would be fed well and make his fortune? After starvation and poor treatment in mines and railroad companies had been the norm, men swarmed to Milwaukee's Western Extension.

Still some of the hardest labor on earth against incredible extremes in weather where fourteen feet of snow was a normal winter occurrence, men wanted one thing — opportunity.

I loved researching, exploring the trail, and writing this story. I loved the heroic stories told on the trail. Including the cameo of the man who gave up everything, including his health for the rest of his life, to save forty-five others humbles me.

Could I do what Edward Pulaski did? Could you? Did you know he invented the firefighters' Pulaski Tool? My heart breaks for what looked on the outside as a failed life. He died scarred inside, his lungs, and outwardly he died as a poor, disabled man. His disabilities caused by saving all those lives. Yet Edward didn't just save those he protected during the firestorm. Edward Pulaski's invention has saved countless lives since then. And he never saw a dime for it. I believe his reward in Heaven is beyond anything we could ever imagine. I hope I can convey even a tiny bit of his stunning bravery. I hope we can all appreciate how much he gave without anything in return.

Come with me, back to 1910, into a sweet romance that battles racism, prejudice, and the unforgiving force of nature that leaves destruction in its path. Come with me to the Flame of the Rockies.

CHAPTER 1

July 4th, 1910

Adair, Idaho — *Deep in the Bitterroot Mountains Milwaukee Railroad Western Extension on the Montana-Idaho Border*

JULIANA HAYES SQUINTED AGAINST THE SUN breaking over the sharp rock outline of the Bitterroot Mountains. Each escaping ray ratcheted up the thermometer in the early Pacific Northwest morning.

Giant cedars looming above eighty-foot white pine should offer refuge and shade. Instead their shadows falling across the rails and platform represented the immobile bars of her prison. In the distance, the forest closed so tightly it looked like rolls of dark green velvet. Such beauty hid the malevolent nature of the area's extreme dangers. As dangerous as some of the men Juliana cautiously avoided since being stranded.

How much longer until she could break out of the

harsh existence that held her captive for over two years?

The deep snows in winter and the fires in summer, only two of the extremes she could do without. The oncoming train puffed out clouds of smoke against a sky so blue and clear it resembled a lake more than the heavens. But she'd ridden that train many times praying they'd make it to the next mining camp through heavy snow and bitter cold. Did there exist another place so wildly inhospitable?

"Anot'er hot day, Mrs. Hayes." The baggage handler lifted his flat cloth cap and rubbed a gray cotton sleeve across his forehead. "Who knew America would be such a hot place?" He flopped the cap back on his head as he waited with her on Adair's small, sturdy platform for the train to sidle up. She'd join the shift change for the mines dotted through the wilderness settlements and narrow, serpentine valley to deliver her quota of baked goods.

"We've never had a summer as hot before, not that I can remember." His foreign accent hard to distinguish all the words.

Was he Austrian, Belgian, Croatian? She didn't ask. He obviously wasn't Chinese or Japanese with his blond hair. She tried not to wrinkle her nose. It was blond, wasn't it? Hard to tell when these men likely bathed only on their day off. He stood tall enough to stick out among the Japanese who mostly inhabited the tent city of Adair nowadays.

She could speak to the weather safely. No more though without encouraging him. "After the avalanches in the spring, I don't think anyone expected this drought."

"I heard da winters here are hard. You do good wi' dem?"

She nodded, avoiding too much conversation. There must be more than seventy different nationalities working on the rails and the mines here on the border of Montana and Idaho. Some nationalities so close they spoke similar languages, only the colors or sometimes a piece of native clothing distinguished them one from another. This mish-mash of humanity from every known continent all with the same hope—to make their fortunes, whether to bring over more family or get rich quick or hide from the law. Money drove these desperate men. Some also desperate for a woman.

His clothing suggested another Austrian. They tended to band together, each of these different nationalities. Keeping familiar languages together helped with communication overall as the foremen were hired because they spoke English and the native language of their crews, sometimes a few more languages or dialects.

The mixed-pidgin varieties were endless, and sometimes humorous, but the pidgin languages helped bridge one group to another unless they clashed. They often clashed. Tempers as hot as the rail spikes in the sun after a day of excruciating cold, wet work deep in the rocky mountainsides. Shivering cold in the depth of summer as she sweated by the oven each day held a fascination for her. Not enough to risk entering the dark abode of miners. As important the sense of togetherness inside a group, ironic how that togetherness habitually incited aggression and animosity toward outsiders. Why couldn't they all just get along? How did they have the energy for savagery?

Juliana did her best to be as neutral and invisible as possible down to wearing dull clothing and keeping her long hair tied up under her baker's scarf. But as a young woman, that worked as well as a queen bee in a hive. She hated developing the stinger that went along with the unwanted attention buzzing around her like soldier bees. But she'd been left with little other protection when her husband died.

Not long now. She calculated her time left based on her weekly pay envelope. She could shed the protective veneer in nine weeks, six days, and twelve hours — give or take the time it took the train to leave the mountains behind. She'd have her trunk on the very next train to Helena without a second glance. There'd be no salt pillar of Juliana Hayes in Adair, Idaho or any other debauched mining town in this forsaken place.

This Austrian, or whatever, was new on the job in a constantly changing mass of men. He'd met her at the brick dome ovens in Adair the last few days to help load a converted mining cart with the staples she baked for the workers up and down the line. At least she could understand most of his English—and he didn't seem to be a Montenegrin, by the look of him. Those vicious men tended to work in Rowland and Taft, on her Tuesday and least favorite route. Why did she have to feed the very men who murdered her husband? A shiver ran through her spine. She'd have to deliver the bread order tomorrow. Each week she considered adding sawdust, or worse, to the dough—and each week she mashed the desire down deep as she punched the bread into submission. Twenty loaves untainted by her dark desire for vengeance.

Vengeance is mine, saith the Lord. She repeated that verse each time the snake's temptation squeezed its coils around her heart.

"I hear said da snow gets deep as the depot roof."

Juliana nodded again and graced the man with a quick, courteous smile careful not to encourage anything. Too nice a response would garner yet another proposal or a lewd proposition. No response and she'd have to lug all four heavy freight baskets onto the train to the next stop on her daily deliveries. Her pay packet from the railroad would be reduced if she cost precious production minutes, she knew from experience when she first started for the Milwaukee Railroad. The company didn't care that she was a new widow. They cared she kept up with her quotas.

"Too bad we don't have a little snow left over." She mumbled as pleasant as possible, under the circumstances. "I hope we don't see a fire season so dangerous again as that one two years ago." She didn't want to relive a summer like that for more reasons than the spot wildfires. Her grief had been as thick as the smoke trapped by the jagged peaks.

"Was bad, ja?"

"Yes."

The engine whistle blew three long shrieks as metal on metal squealed a high-pitched complaint braking the train to a stop. The nearness of the rocky mountain slopes amplified the sounds. The conductor, in overalls and brimmed summer hat, leaned out the caboose porch. He leapt onto the wooden platform and ran nimbly along the train before it had a chance to stop, bellowing, "All 'board! Let's be movin', folks." He inspected the waiting cargo, including the amount Juliana brought aboard. "Mornin', Widow Hayes."

"Good morning, Mr. Kelly." She handed him a couple of buttermilk biscuits filled with apple butter wrapped and in cheesecloth. The conductor often missed meals for train delays. "There's one for the engineer also."

"Yer a good woman, ya are." He tipped his hat and strode at a fast pace toward the front. "Johnnie, we been visited by the Angel of Adair! Looky the size of them biscuits!" Only he called her that and only he was allowed. The older man, stronger than his wrinkles led one to believe, had shoved more than his share of miscreants off the train for interfering in her duties.

Johnnie Mackedon tooted out his thanks on the whistle. One of his signatures. Stay long enough and each engineer could be recognized by the way they pulled the train whistle.

She laughed and gave him a quick wave as she called out, "You're welcome, Johnnie."

The burly handler lifted the heavier basket laden with oversized loaves and walked with Juliana toward the steps leading into the first passenger car.

As he shifted to pass another up to the top step, he said, "Mizz Hayes, I been meanin'—"

Juliana made a show of focusing on raising her skirt to climb the steps. Three days it took him. Must be a record. "Oh look, the front seats are open. Mr. Kelly keeps them clear for me, you know." Prime space to settle in with her tasty cargo that still wafted the fresh-baked aroma of oat bran, whole wheat, and honey all around her.

The rich scent of baked goods helped to mask the constant smell of the mine muck and men. She always rode in front. First on and off to keep deliveries moving, and the unwanted scent of unwashed bodies blown behind her by the open windows. In the front, she avoided eye contact. They might approach her with odious offers, but none would dare take a Milwaukee Railroad baker's chosen space. The company provided the best grub in the country for their workforce, supplementing the regular camp cooks. Bellies held priority until full. Then it switched to other appetites. Appetites she refused to fill.

All eyes devoured her as if she were a Sunday cinnamon raisin bun. How unfriendly did she have to be to protect herself? It seemed the colder she behaved the harder some men tried. She'd heard the dares and the bets and chose to ignore them. One at a time, she could rebuff the advances.

"Mizz—"

"I don't want to keep you from your other freight or we'll both get docked for delaying the shift change." Not today. She didn't want to be targeted by teeming crews snatching up the handful of women as wives or worse. No, she couldn't stomach it today of all days. She lifted the nearest bread crate and stowed it.

"Ma'am, the party tonight, if you're of the mind—" His voice soft, pleading.

He might even be a nice man. But Juliana didn't want a man here, nice or otherwise. She took the last crate from him and backed away, setting the bread on the front seat beside her. The length hung well beyond the edge. With those stacked on the floor near her feet, another across the aisle, they formed a sort of protective fencing. A small fortress protecting her personal space.

The whistle blew, sounding departure. She couldn't give him a hair of a chance to spit the rest of the words out. "I'll bring a few loaves of hearty dark rye in the morning. I know that's a favorite with the wild onion and venison sandwiches. I heard your bunkhouse got a big buck the other day. Maybe a trade for some meat?" The extra work would be worth it if she could supplement her pantry and not spend out of her savings. And steer the conversation away from what she knew came next.

"Good, ja, to be sure. Would you—"

The conductor pushed through the entry. "Get on back to loading, Jack." He jabbed an elbow into the baggage man's ribs, whose name was something more like Jacques, if one could get the accent right. "The Widow Hayes got 'er job and yous got yers." He stood with fists on his hips. "Move it, man, get those supplies loaded and leave room for them pack horses!"

A moment later, Juliana escaped the first proposal of the day by luck and by golly. At least he'd tried to be nice. Three stops to dispatch last night's labor, and a basket of buttermilk biscuits for the highest weekly production, then the ride back to Adair. Tomorrow she'd deliver to Rowland and the cycle would continue six days out of seven. The Rowland baker from down the line would overlap schedules for her one day off on Sunday, as the others did for the all the mining camps stretched through the long valley along the tracks. Juliana rarely saw the other women as they worked each other's days off. Most had marital and family duties to catch up. Each baked for her camp and three to four more that either didn't have an oven and baker or she only worked part-time due to other responsibilities.

She slid against the seat-back savoring the air flowing in from the window. So many days lately the air stood still as a deer at the crack of a twig. Her only relief came from the train window. Juliana split her schedule and baked half her quota well before dawn during the summer to avoid the intense heat of the huge brick ovens in the late afternoon, the hottest part of the day in the Idaho panhandle.

She had little chance of avoiding several more marriage—or unmentionable—invitations with the significance of the holiday for citizens and immigrants alike. She smoothed the worn white apron over her tan cotton work skirt. She'd have on black still, but that brought the men out of the tunnels and mines as much as the whiskey called them to the saloons. A black dress meant a woman had no man, fair game in this most beautiful of desolate places. Mary, a new baker, had been carried to the preacher within days of arriving last summer. Carried. That miner wasn't taking a chance of cold feet or bridal theft. Bridal theft could get a man killed in these parts as much as having the precious commodity of a bride, if she were particularly desirable. Most respected marriage, though they'd line up to pay respects at any married man's funeral in hopes of walking the new widow right past her home and into theirs. Women like Astrid picked a new husband quickly, especially if she had children to support. These mountains could be ruthless in both weather and wild animals. Though a lost child in the woods could still prove a bit of humanity existed even if the celebration caused havoc afterward.

This summer poor Mary nursed a newborn and baked. Mary managed to give away one of her days to another miner's wife, a previous canary, that wanted honest work rather than the bawdy house her husband had found her in.

Not me, Lord. Be it your will, I'm getting out of here come end of September! I am not raising a family here, if you ever grace me with a good man again let it be in a city! Strike that. I'd rather just have a city life. If it be Your will.

Some days Juliana felt more like a lone stalk of grain in a herd of buffalo bulls all snorting and ramming one another. After this summer ended, she'd have enough to move on before the harsh winter hit again. She'd take this very train into Helena, Montana, the Queen City of the Rockies, and never look back. Maybe she'd continue to Minneapolis or keep going as far East as Chicago. With the mastery of mass baking she'd gained, her own pastry shop would serve cookies, cakes, and anything to break the monotony of wheat bread and sour dough, four days a week, cinnamon raisin or another sweet bread on Saturdays for their Sunday meals, and the highly-prized dark rye to the weekly winners of extra rations.

Only a short ride between towns, the train wove beside the St. Joe river, flowing low from the heat and lack of rain, and around the wide bend before pulling into Kyle. Deliver into the depot, climb on the next train to Stetson. Deliver, climb on the next train to Avery. Then home to Adair to start the dough for tomorrow. The cycle didn't slow. Mix dough, bake bread, deliver bread to miners and railroaders. Keep them working.

Juliana stared out the window at the white pine, cedar, and river flashing past as they rode deeper into the rugged realm. Why couldn't she have fallen in love with a man who would stay in the city the first time? She could have avoided this day when everyone else would celebrate the country's independence, it was the second anniversary of her husband's death.

"Get outta my way!" The shouts erupted several rows from the front.

"I got dibs!"

Juliana rolled her eyes heavenward, but didn't bother to look at the skirmish. She already knew what caused the fight. She plunked her elbow on the window ledge and dropped her chin into it, staring at the passing landscape. Nine weeks and six days...

CHAPTER 2

LUKAS TOOK A HEADCOUNT OF HIS NEWLY hired crew as they boarded the back of the railcar from the Kyle platform. He breathed in relief as he followed them inside. He'd pick up a few more extras from the other foreman, if they had them to spare, and head back to Rowland. Better to be prepared for attrition. Any given day a man walked off the job without a word.

A whiff of fresh bread floated from the front of the car, wafting in the air, between bodies pushing for seating. He closed his eyes and inhaled deeply. He'd like one good day this month. Just one. It'd be topped off with a hunk of that bread and the ability to concentrate on the actual job rather than refilling empty positions for the company. His stomach rumbled. Bad coffee reheated from last night didn't make the best breakfast. Perhaps the baker would have a bite to spare in her bundles?

As the crowded aisle diminished, one lummox

shoved another backward. "I ain't givin' way! She ain't got a man an' I ain't got a woman. I'm tired o' spendin' money on canaries."

"An' you ain't getting' betwixt she an' me!" The targeted victim, righted by his buddy behind him, used the upward momentum, and shoved back sending his opponent flying across two other men.

Shouts and curses turned to bets on the winner as the crew tossed the rivals in the middle.

"That don't make you the one she wants!"

"Well, she don't want you, smelly—"

In less time than the breadth of a horsehair, the first man fisted and decked the guy.

Not ducking out, the punched man recovered, again with the assistance of a buddy catching and releasing him with forward momentum into battle.

The rest of the crew leaned over seats, egging the two on, cheering for their favorite, and passing money to the man nearest the fight who acted as the bank.

By the time Lukas made it through the tangle of bodies blocking his progress, the culprits were on the floor trying to strangle one another over a woman. Not the first fight he'd seen since females were as rare in this rugged country as trout in the low river. The job challenged the strongest men physically, mentally, and spiritually.

After a month as the hiring foreman, he'd discovered the most grueling job, his, was keeping the mines running against the constant loss of manpower from giving up or getting beat or moving on. Men could take the hard work. They could handle the extremes in temperature. But the lack of womankind wreaked havoc in a way he couldn't have fathomed when he agreed to the contract. Men forged the roads, built the towns, answered the call of adventure. But women—they tamed hearts, settled men, and created civilization.

The production reports took backseat to order, discipline, and the act of production. Two months of reports from the last foreman never happened. Now he knew why. His first had yet to be finished for the company. But if he lost any more men, he'd be down in the mines working an empty shift again. Though he'd earned respect by doing it.

Now this mess—before the day even started—he pushed the gawkers in the inner circle back into their seats, a firm hand on a shoulder if one protested. They took one look at who dared and backed down. Many here stood taller than average and sported physiques built out of years on farms, railroads, mines, or prison. All came for the opportunity, but few boasted the equivalent of his height and frame. The epitome of a European man who'd worked hard through his boyhood. That fact alone stopped many problems. He had the additional benefit of an excellent education and leadership skills. Then his deep voice cinched it for the rest.

Lukas grabbed a handful of shirt collar and hauled the bigger brute up in one yank. The man landed on his feet staring up into his foreman's darkened glare. "You will stop."

The other contender leapt to his feet and launched forward, fists primed. Lukas extended a flat palm with such force toward the oncoming attacker, he knocked the wind out of him. "You will also stop."

Never once did he raise his voice above a low growl as he spoke in his native language. His height alone commanded attention. But accompanied by the muscular body of heavy labor since childhood cowed most would-be challengers. Add the resonant baritone, that when raised in worship filled a church with beauty song. That same vocal quality, directed in discipline, shook the recipient to the core. As head foreman, in charge of men pushed past human endurance, decency in the ranks didn't last long. Lukas had no choice but to be half father and half bouncer. What he couldn't afford to be was too close of a friend, not among these intense conditions. Enough to build connection and enough command to build respect. Something his father had taught him about managing their holdings while tutoring Lukas to take over.

"What was this about?" He asked the man whose scruff he still held.

"Her." He pointed at the baker in the front row, wooden bins of bread all around her making a kind of blockade. She faced forward with a stiffened spine, pointedly ignoring the scene not far behind her, arms wrapped tightly around her torso. Did she know the fight was over her or couldn't she understand the language?

One of the miners nearby laughed, and explained, "Ain't no big deal. Someone's always makin' a play for her. She ain't givin' the likes o' those two no never mind. Gotta be a rich man to catch a gal like that one.

I'll get me rich and then get that gal for my personal canary."

The fellows around him slapped him on the back. One said, "You better be gone then. Her last man didn't survive. What makes you different?"

"You just try me." He came up off his seat.

Lukas backed him down still holding the first offender's collar.

The bakers, hired directly by the Milwaukee Railroad, were hard to find and a difficult position to refill. If Lukas wanted bread for his crews, that lady needed protection from the men she had to feed.

He switched to English hoping the woman would understand he had everything under control. "You will all leave the baker alone. If not, you will answer to me." He narrowed his eyes, looked at each man, and asked, "Do we understand each other?"

Lukas caught a flicker of movement in the front row. Had she glanced over her shoulder?

"Ja." The one who could still speak squeaked out as he nodded.

Letting the man go, he pointed at the bench several rows back. Then he turned to the smaller culprit. "Und?"

He nodded.

Lukas released him.

The fellow sputtered, wheezed, and worked his way down the aisle doubled-over to sit as far away from Lukas as he could get.

Lukas stared down the entire compartment. Then he shook his head. One perfect day. This wouldn't be it. He searched for a seat, catching hold of one he passed to balance as the train swayed around a bend. All full until he reached the front.

"May I?" He asked the pretty bread baker. The company of a sweet soul with kind words would do a lot to ease the stress today. Surely, she'd be kind after what he'd done for her.

She turned from the window, sized him up with caramel brown eyes in a flash that rocked him as hard as dynamite blasting a mining shaft. "No."

Eyes he hadn't seen in the month he'd ridden behind the baker or in a different car dealing with new men, paperwork, and supplies. He'd caught a glimpse of freckles across glowing cheeks and honey-colored hair under her baker's scarf. He'd seen her from a distance. He knew of her. Until now, he'd no idea what she looked like. Only the rumor that she was a looker.

Sometimes Lukas missed the train altogether when he had to roust employees out of a bordello, likely still drunk. But those eyes needed studying. He understood now what the men fought over. A chance to capture the light in those eyes—or to be the man that put it there.

The train ratcheted around another curve jostling Lukas into a giant basket, almost spilling its contents. He righted it, without losing a loaf or the perfect packing order, and then held out a hand. "Terribly sorry, Miss—"

"It's Mrs." The woman held up her hand displaying a plain gold band on her fourth finger. She reached across the basket and pulled it back from Lukas. Then turned away to the window without another word.

A choked snicker transformed into a cough when Lukas turned to look.

The miner fixed his eyes on the floor suddenly fascinated by his muddy, bedraggled boots.

More now than any time, he had to establish authority with the replacements or risk costly disrespect. That could mean lives. Lengthening his scrutiny with disapproval until the man inched toward the window like a naughty puppy. Expanding to include the others in the vicinity, he quelled any further laughter intended to minimize his leadership. Sometimes he felt sorry for his past teachers. This must be similar to how they felt with a bunch of unruly adolescents.

"My apologies, ma'am." He lifted the basket off the bench across the aisle. "Would you mind if I held this for you while I sit here?"

She glanced over her shoulder, took in the packed passenger car, and then at him. "That would be fine as I see no other option."

"I'm Lukas Filips." He thumbed toward the other passengers, half already snoring. "They shouldn't bother you again."

"Yous got that right." The conductor said as he arrived, coming up through the train. "I ain't got the time to be runnin' through my train to keep the peace." He shook his head. "From now on, any o' your lot rides an' yous gonna be ridin' or y'all be walkin'!"

Lukas furrowed his brow. "I can't—"

The conductor shrugged. "Suit yerself." He leaned down toward the woman and peered out the window at the thick brush along the river. "Guess them boys want to work up a good appetite fer yer baked goods since they'll be addin' a couple miles walk through the brambles." He chuckled as he straightened, but that low laugh held a tone of finality.

She rewarded him with a raised eyebrow. "Could make for an uncommonly pleasant ride, Mr. Kelly."

"You know I have to keep my men working. I can't—"

"No siree, ain't gonna tell yous yer business. Jes tryin' to help as best I can in the circumstance." He held his palms up. "You 'n me, we got our jobs. Mine is to get my passengers, cargo, and the baker ladies to their destinations. When yer fellas make my job harder, ain't much of a leap fer me. I like her cookin' more than I like bustin' up a boxin' match ever' mornin' and noon. Get me?"

One more log to roll out of the way in the jam piling up. He'd have to ride from Roland and make the loop every day to ensure the early crew arrived until their bunkhouse, closer to the mine, was completed.

"What if we strike a deal? I ride for a short time. If there's no problem, we call it solved." The hour, plus travel time, would cost him in yet later reports. But if helping this one very pretty woman helped him manage his crew better then so be it.

"Knew he'd see reason, Widow Hayes. Yous let me know if you got any problem. I ain't got no problem bannin' that bunch." The conductor pulled out his pocket watch. "Back to it then." He flipped it closed as he left Lukas and the caramel-eyed widow staring at one another.

He curbed the desire to shout, speaking low enough for the two of them to hear. "How am I supposed to get any work done or manage my crews?"

Her eyes widened like an oasis emerging from the sands, and just as surprising, "You think I've no work to do? It's your men that often delay me." She rose with hands on hips. The train jockeyed for its position, snaking 'round another bend. "I have bread to get to—" Another quick jolt to the left and the beauty flopped down on her bench as if the hand of God brushed against Widow Hayes, plopping her in a most unladylike fashion to finish the conversation. "Never mind." She turned away. "I don't want to talk about it."

"Wait, Widow Hayes." He slid a basket off the seat and sat beside her. "How do my men make you late?"

She stared at him. "How would you manage in this female-starved environment, if you were me?"

Shouldn't she know the answer? Isn't marriage obvious with all these wolves howling at her door? "I don't understand." Maybe it was a nuance in the English language he had yet to learn, though his education had been thorough in English, Russian, French, Croatian, Italian, and his own mother tongue. "What do you mean?"

"Was that not you breaking up the fight?" She tilted her head. "That's only one example. When that kind of thing happens, I'm often blocked from getting deliveries through the crowd and miss a train. Or, heaven help me, I get stopped just for a little chat." Her voice mimicked the gruffness in many of the men. "As if I don't know what that means. What do I have to do to avoid all the manhandling?"

"I—"

"If I wanted to work in a bawdy house, that's where

I'd be. I've chosen to bake." She folded her arms. "That's all."

"I—"

"Of course, the drunks on the train each day that make it harder to get on and off or try to follow me home has to be the worst. Then again, you did say you would personally stop the poor behavior. Why don't you tell me how you'll do that if you aren't on board?"

Would she breathe and let him speak? For a woman who didn't want to talk about it, she said a lot.

"Well?"

Oh, his turn. "I'll be on board. My men will not bother you."

"Fine." She arched a brow that proved she didn't believe in the possibility or his promise. The train pulled into the makeshift station at Stetson. "If you'll hand the basket down, please, I'll be right back. Unless you'd extend your protection into the depot?"

He assessed the silent car. Not one man dared break a grin. But all eyes were on him. If he wanted to show these men how to behave, now he had the chance.

"Ma'am." Lukas stood with her, stepped aside to allow her to pass, and followed her off the train carrying the massive basket. He heard a low whistle and then, "Look at that, will ya? I ain't sure if'n the Widow Hayes tamed the foreman, or the foreman is taming the Widow Hayes."

"I'll take that bet." And the ruckus started, money passing back and forth, plainly visible through the windows to anyone on the depot platform.

Lukas closed his eyes for a brief moment and breathed deeply. He could and would be a gentleman.

He could and would be the example the men needed. Hopefully, she hadn't heard that last bit in English.

She turned back toward the noise, studied the apparent nonsense, and said, "I'm not sure you'll be able to manage that lot. Perhaps you won't want to get back on the train either, Mr. Filips."

His hackles raised at her challenge, and he drew his brows together. First the conductor and now a woman he'd never met before. "You'll leave that to me."

With this many men vying for her hand, surely, she could simply solve the problem by picking one before he'd have to do much more. Especially since she no longer wore widow's weeds. "However, it seems you should simply choose a husband. Plenty will be at the celebrations tonight. You can take your pick."

The widow spun on her heel before she crossed the depot threshold. One hand on her hip and one pointing right into his chest. "You hear me good. I will never, not ever, will not even consider a ruffian the likes of these!" She flicked her hand outward toward the audience. Her eyes narrowed, "No train man or miner or any man… no, no, no! Why can't you all leave me alone?"

He'd hold his hands out to show he'd meant no offense, but they were full of her bread. Then he realized the entire train could see him get an earful. Could she make his job any harder today?

"And you! You're just like all of them, aren't you?"

"My bet is on the widow, Foreman Filips!" At least that jest was in his mother tongue. Laughter roared out of the open windows behind him.

But from the irritated expression on her face, she

likely caught the gist anyway. Did she speak more than English?

She tightened her lips and went inside.

Yes. She could make it harder. Lukas growled under his breath as he went inside the cooler log building, dropped the load where she directed, and walked the lady back to the train in silence.

CHAPTER 3

THE TRAIN CHUGGED DOWN THE TRACK TO THE next stop. They repeated the delivery in near silence, only speaking for directions and to acknowledge the other out of curt courtesy. His men watching every detail.

Juliana settled into her seat. He'd helped her finish the delivery even though she'd yelled at him in front of all those men. Embarrassed him, after he'd already broken up a fist fight. After he'd agreed to keep her safe, on a daily basis. The guilt poured over her heart and festered like yeast in sugar water.

"I'm sorry." The words barely audible. She cleared her throat. "I'm sorry I snapped at you." Juliana snuck a sideways, upward glance across the aisle at his surprisingly clean russet hair and stoic profile. A fine-looking face, for a miner, she allowed with a tad bit of realism. She liked his clean-shaven chin with the small cleft. Most men around the mines wore long, unkempt beards. Half of those stained with tobacco.

He inclined his head without turning to look at Juliana. "Accepted."

He still clenched his jaw, a small muscle popping in and out. "You've accepted my apology, but have you forgiven me?"

No response.

"Mr. Filips?"

He searched her face. "You have made my job more difficult," he gestured back toward his crew, "...but yes I choose to forgive you."

She smiled, and when he smiled back, Juliana's heart warmed. Of course, the sunshine streaming in through the window had everything to do with feeling overheated. It certainly wasn't the handsome mining foreman whose gray-blue eyes twinkled at her like sunlight winking on a lake. Juliana slid a finger around the high collar of her shirt blouse. She needed a cold drink of water.

Their mutual smiles brought attention. One of the men who'd been fighting yelled toward the front. "You oughta get in line, Foreman. Ain't no cause for you to swoop in and steal the girl from them what's been tryin' all summer."

Mr. Filips turned, his arm across the back of his bench. "The man drew the short straw on smarts." He first said quietly to Juliana causing a giggle to burst from her. He gave her the most intense momentary stare as if the sound of her laugh entranced him. Then he raised his baritone, "Rowdy, I know you need this job since you've been let go from two other foreman. You want a third boot?"

That sent a guffaw around the men who'd boarded at the new stops along the ride.

The depth of that look, penetrating behind her wall, sent her scurrying to reinforce the safety zone. She mentally built a heavier barrier to his masculinity.

"I'm grateful for your help today and your willingness to help in the future." She gathered the baskets and stacked them on the bench to keep distance between them. He'd done nothing untoward, but the way he looked at her sent sparklers to her stomach. Since she had no plans of attending the holiday celebration this evening, she didn't want to see fireworks in a new relationship either. She needed to get home and not dream of a tall handsome man when she slept away the afternoon heat. She needed to finish the first rising and then bake tonight. All the railroaders and miners would be busy celebrating. She wouldn't have to fend off anyone between the oven and her quarters while they were at the saloons. Enough celebration for her. Then she'd prep the next set of batches for the ovens after the stragglers wandered through to the bunkhouses. She'd be done in time for the baggageman to tote it all to the platform, ready for the train.

"Mrs. Hayes, we're going to be riding for at least an hour every morning, maybe more. Would it be a better idea to become friends?"

Juliana wished she could say yes to his intriguing man. The risk outweighed the momentary relief. Good things come to those who wait, she told herself. She was waiting for a life outside of the camps. "It's not better for me." She swallowed at his disappointed expression. Not wanting to be friends would hurt anyone. With as much courtesy as she dared, Juliana apologized. "I'm sorry. But you don't know what I've been through."

"I don't. But friends can listen and ease the burden."

He had a genuine demeanor and a handsome face... and actual manners. His offer tempted Juliana beyond her expectations.

At the roar of laughter over a ribald comment, she retreated from the offer. These men were transients and so was she. Her lonely life here would be done, gone by September. Nine weeks and six days left till freedom from camp life, by her calculations. She'd have been here just over three years then. The one year Hayes had promised and then the two on her own. Long enough to have earned a better life, albeit without the husband and children she'd imagined. But she'd be established. Then building a new life would come naturally.

"I'm not in need of a listening ear."

"Ah, you already have someone to share your thoughts."

His words drilled a little light through her wall. To have normal conversation about the day? About her dreams? She tightened her heart. Not now. Not so close to her escape.

"Surely you can see how it doesn't work with the transient nature of your business." Other men had paid her kindnesses, she'd responded at first. All it did was encourage them to try and win a wife or a wanton. They all had ulterior motives. Men wanted their houses cleaned, their bread baked, and their—needs met. All expectations without the pay or the freedom she wanted. Even her sweet husband had changed once he'd brought her to this dismal camp life. He'd planned to make enough money to build her a house in Spokane.

"How can that be true?"

"It is true, for me." She lifted her chin at his scowl of disbelief. "Mr. Filips, it is true for me."

"Will you at least tell me why? I only mean to—"

She had to tell him or make it the business of everyone. Juliana lowered her voice. "Because I am not staying. I want no strings to this place. When I leave, I am not coming back. Though it's not likely, I do not want to miss anyone here."

"Many people move on. But friendships, we need friends. We need others." He reached out to touch her hand to console or convince.

Juliana pulled her hand back as if a bear tried to maul her. "I do not need anyone else in my life."

"Then you don't need me to help you each morning?" He sat back and crossed his feet. "That will make my life so much easier."

Her eyes flared wide, and despite the suffocating heat, she blanched. "You promised."

"Ah, but only as long as I was needed." He gave her a polite smile. "You have said I am not. I'll let Conductor Kelly know when we reach the next stop."

"No, I didn't mean it that way." Glancing over her shoulder, half the men snored from working all night and the day crew seemed suddenly fascinated by the conversation from the front of the car. Panic swirled in her throat. Left to their own devices, she'd be fighting off continual problems again each time she boarded the train.

"I'm sure you'll be fine. After all, you said you'd been doing this a long time."

Yes, she had and it grew harder by the day. The transitory nature of the Bitterroot mining camps brought out the roughest in the male species. Many were here out of desperation. Some running from the law, more than she cared to think about, and some after the next big mother lode. Most lacked the common civility of citified folk. The kind of people she'd chosen to leave behind when...it didn't matter. What's done is done. She dropped her gaze into her lap and twisted the gold wedding band. This entire time since she'd been widowed, she hadn't had as peaceful a delivery route. Pursing her lips, Juliana braced to admit it.

"Hey, widder woman, you gonna be at the party tonight?" The voice called from the very back, over the noise of the train. "I got a spot on yer dance card, ya hear?"

"I got her dance card right here!" Another yelled in response.

"Oh yeah, Jonesy?" One more joined in the taunting, "Who needs a dance card? I got these here two arms to sweep her off her feet and right to the preacher. She'll fit right nice in 'em and we'll see if anybody else can take her out once I got her." He struck a pose showing his biceps.

Gritting her teeth, she closed her eyes, and then heaved out the frustration in a heavy sigh. Maybe it wasn't just the men from Rowland she wanted to feed sawdust!

The foreman, in a lithe move, stood facing the men.

"There will be no sweeping Mrs. Hayes off her feet!" He thundered out the words.

Juliana couldn't help herself. She stared in astonishment at her protector. Any other time, that phrase would have sounded comical. Somehow Foreman Filips made it sound downright heroic.

"If there is a dance card, it belongs to me and me only."

"You stakin' a claim on that gal, Foreman?"

He looked at her, then at Jonesy. "*Ona je moja žena.*"

Except for the part where he claimed her all of a sudden. Now what?

The car went silent a moment. Then Jonesy said, "I gots ya. She's already goin' wit' choo. You been up there sweet talkin' her all the while, h'ain't ya?"

"What d'ya gotta do 'round these parts ta get a break?" Another groused.

"Figures. Gotta be management fer a woman likes o' her to go sparkin'."

Juliana tried to take it as a compliment. But words like that weren't meant to compliment. These men acted like wolves over an elk calf. She chose to keep her dignity and sat up straighter while snapping face forward. How did she end up with the pack leader?

"Fine, then." Jonesy gave way. "If she goes with you tonight, I'll find me another. But I'll be watchin' fer my chance, ya hear?"

"She's going with me tonight. Or shall we have a private discussion when the train stops?"

"When ya put it like that."

"Wouldn't wanna cause no trouble."

"I got my eye on another missy."

The whistle blew train pulled into the Adair platform, letting the men off to their intended destination of either mines or temporary barracks. Foreman Filips had not sat back down. He'd folded his arms, planted his feet, and blocked the way to the front exit going by Juliana. The car emptied fast. No one seemed to dawdle.

She waited for all the men to clear the platform. "I can't you know." She looked up from the seat. "I have to work." Tonight she did not want to celebrate.

"Well, Mrs. Hayes, it's like this. I can't do my first hour of work each day until I ride you around this track. So it seems fair that to make my job easier, you'll show up for an hour tonight with me to keep all those hounds off the scent of an unattached female and their minds on the job so I might finally finish overdue reports."

"What did you say to them? The part I couldn't understand."

He looked a bit sheepish. "I said you were my girl."

"You — but I'm not anyone's girl."

The whistle blew for departure.

"What's it to be? We help each other so we both can do our jobs or are we done here and now?"

She opened her mouth, but closed it at his serious expression. "I'll see you tonight, Mr. Filips."

"It's Lukas." He hunkered down near her while taking the stack of bread bins.

His hands rested for a moment on the top of the baskets, near her knees, while those blue-gray eyes watched and waited.

His nearness the closest she'd allowed a man in two years. Her mouth went dry. "Mr. Filips, I—"

"Lukas, or no one will believe you."

She nodded. Then with a light tap to her collar, she said, "Juliana."

He broke into one of those heart-flipping grins. "Juliana. I'll pick you up about seven, as long as the train is on time."

He carried the empty baskets to the platform, placing them into her waiting handcart that now sat in the shade of the depot. "Maybe then you'll at least allow me to become a friend. I could use one outside of the crews, you know."

She watched him run, swing up onto the train as it chugged away toward Grand Forks, Rowland, and Taft.

"No, you of all men cannot be my friend. And not on this day." She had to find a way to keep him at a distance. He was different, almost cultured though he spoke English with quite a romantic accent. Not one she recognized. Lukas Filips behaved like a gentleman, a rare breed in these mountain mining operations.

She pushed her oversized handcart toward the path. What was he doing here?

CHAPTER 4

JULIANA PUNCHED DOWN THE DOUGH. "A dance. Like I have anything to wear to a dance."

She shoved back dangling hair that escaped its updo with her wrist. Folding, kneading, and then shaping the mound of honey wheat bread helped her work out the worry.

She squeezed off a handful, rolled it into a ball, and smashed it flat. Then she set it aside for a few moments to finish dividing the rest into greased bowls for rising. Each huge bowl had its own damp cheesecloth laid over top to keep out the bugs and keep the dough from drying out as it rose, then she set them on the table.

Picking up her small piece, she fried it in butter in a cast iron skillet. A simple dinner of fry bread, honey, and a few garden vegetables would suffice until Jacques traded for the extra loaves for some venison tomorrow.

Juliana had sold her pretty dresses long since to build up savings for her escape. It'd take more than her trousseau to open a pastry shop. She owned four dresses, not including her wedding suit. Two skirts for work, one for Sunday best, and her widow's weeds that cost her too much and proved to be wasted. The black skirt and blouse hung on pegs acting as the wardrobe on the back wall of her cabin. Could she dress up the skirt if she wore a white blouse with it?

The sun wouldn't set till past ten, though the shadows would be long thanks to the ragged mountain tops and tall trees. That skirt was the only clean one. Laundry day wasn't until tomorrow when she could get to the river because she didn't have extra loaves to bake on Wednesdays. Juliana also avoided the men who didn't want to pay for baths on Saturdays. She assessed the one she wore. Covered in flour and the dregs of dough on the sleeve, she couldn't wear it either. None would dry fast enough with the time she had left.

There was one other option. The ruffled shirtwaist from the walking suit she left home in, when she married.

Walking slowly to the small bedroom space behind the blanket, Juliana opened the cedar trunk at the foot of the cast iron bed. She moved aside the winter down quilt and lifted out the purple velvet jacket trimmed with matching purple cording and golden buttons. She ran her hand over the softness that rivaled finely milled cake flour. She draped it over the edge of the trunk. Though white as the others, the shirtwaist's tiny pleats layered one another with delicate lace around the waist and bodice.

Memories of trembling in anticipation while she fought the small seed pearl buttons for that lovely afternoon party brought the next bittersweet remembrance. The day of her first kiss. Would wearing the delicately made blouse to tonight's sham spoil the sweetness?

She looked at the soiled clothing in the basket. Like her choice to marry, some decisions brought value beyond the cost. One year with Holmes had been worth it. One night wearing this outfit could likely ease the next nine weeks. Wearing her memories could bring her solace and peace, too. One last sweep of her hand across the fabric sealed her choice. She lifted a sleeve to her cheek as if saying goodbye to the past. Future freedom meant more than an outfit.

Decision made, Juliana rinsed away the day and washed her hair in cool rose water. She left her thick hair down, pulled back into a dark pink ribbon matching her skirt, to finish drying or she'd be chilled in the middle of the night when the mountain air turned colder for a few hours. Pink skirt pressed, white ruffled top, and polished black kid leather walking boots. She smoothed her long skirt, longer than the ankle length work wardrobe, a little self-conscious of the difference since almost two years passed. No one would notice they were a few years out of style here. But they'd notice she wore such rich colors.

At his knock, she startled. Did she have to continue this farce for the entire time or could they relax once they'd given the impression of being sweet on each other tonight at this event?

Rather than invite him into her private space, Juliana went outside. No need to go that far. There were few left in this area of the camp to notice. She raised her eyes as she crossed the threshold stopped mid-step. Lukas' clean blue shirt, denims, and freshly brushed back dark hair smelled of soap and fresh mountain air. She didn't want to like both, but did. Heaven help her, she definitely did.

"Goodness, you certainly wash up well. Not to say you needed a bath..." She didn't know how to do this. "I'm sorry. I'm embarrassed."

Amusement danced around his lips. "Good evening, Juliana." His voice as luscious and smooth as whipped honey butter on a slice of fresh-out-of-the-oven steamy bread.

Her breath caught. Lonely. She'd been very lonely. That's all these awkward feelings were. She cleared her throat. "Good evening, Lukas." Why did her voice sound more like a croaking frog?

"You look," he paused and blinked. "Quite beautiful. Like a wild mountain rose."

He made it easy for her to smile. "Thank you."

"Aside from our plan, I'm proud to escort you to the Independence Day dance."

Proud, goodness. Something was very different about Lukas Filips besides the fact he bathed more than once a week. Juliana took his proffered elbow and walked through the makeshift wood and canvas town that once held more than four hundred men. Over half of the people moved to other mines for the competitive pay. Adair had a few logging crews, but the mine didn't need the same roll call.

"This camp never built up with decent buildings, except one or two. I find it ironic your cabin and the Loop Saloon seem to be the best built. There are other possible living arrangements. What keeps you here rather than one of the better built towns?"

She saw what he saw. Broken down two-by-fours with canvas torn and not repaired on many empty sites. But she saw what he didn't—less men to fend off. Less worry over whether she'd be grabbed unaware while baking to fill those bellies. And then she saw the sadness of it all. The death of a town when the work or mine came to an end. If this one closed, she'd move to the next as long as it wasn't Rowland or Taft.

"The logging helps some stay. Enough I don't fear a bear or wolves. Few enough I fear the men less here than when they congregate in droves needing to prove themselves."

"What do you do for amusement when you're not baking?"

"I attend chapel, read, and plan my future." Juliana reminded him, "I haven't needed to build a big life here because I'm not staying."

A short break from the drudgery would give her the ability to finish this trial well. Tonight, the curtain opened on the final act in the tragedy. But what had been would not be her future. She trusted the Lord would use what she'd been through for her good. Hope sang in her heart as they waited the few minutes for the train heading to the East Portal YMCA, a few miles up the track. She would have her happy ending, just not the true love in all the fairy tales of childhood.

CHAPTER 5

THE PIANO JANGLED ANOTHER UPBEAT TUNE along with East Portal's best fiddler joined by other musicians from up and down the valley. Lukas held out his hand. "Would you care to dance another jig?"

"Could we sit this one out? I feel like I've had enough in this heat."

He noticed the fatigue around her eyes. "How about a little punch and then I get you home. I think we've made our point."

She gave him a grateful nod. "That would be perfect."

As he returned from the punch table carrying much needed drinks, she reached out for the cup, thanking him. "I have enjoyed myself. It's just been a long day with a long week ahead."

He covered her fingers with his palm. "It's been an honor to spend a little time with you." He held her eyes with his. "Maybe we can get together more before you go."

"Maybe." She whispered as she took a sip of the red punch. Her lashes fluttered, shading those pretty eyes. "But I think—"

"Hey, buddy, you gonna share that canary?" A new fellow, with a friendly overly loud Scottish accent, clapped his hand on Lukas' shoulder.

Lukas brushed off his hand. "Mrs. Hayes is not a woman for hire."

His words slurred together from both alcohol and heavy brogue. "Sure, she is. That bunch over there told me so." He thumbed over at the corner where several men who'd ridden the train earlier in the day enjoyed the joke on the unsuspecting logger. "Said I needed to get on her dance card." He stumbled against Lukas, sending his full glass of punch flying out of his hand. The cup spun at their feet as if whirling to its own tune.

Lukas shook his head keeping his eyes fixed on the intruder, not daring to back down, but held his temper. He may be heading toward a headache in the morning, but it was an obvious accident. "I'm telling you they're pulling your leg. Get on your way now."

"I wan' on her dance card." His slurring deepened as did his tone of belligerence.

Lukas went nose-to-nose with him. "Listen, there is no dance card. The lady is with me."

"I'll hear it from the canary first. She can speak for herself."

"I've said it nicely. The lady is not a—"

Juliana put a hand on his bicep and tugged, not budging him a bit. "Lukas, let's leave."

In that moment, the drunk grabbed at Juliana's

waist getting a fistful of lace that lined the tiny pleating design. "Gimme a lil smooch."

Before he could plaster a wet kiss on her, Lukas gripped the man's wrist and twisted him away. But in the process, Juliana's ruffles ripped off ruining her blouse. The drunk swung wide, shredded ruffles between his knuckles, and punched at Lukas.

Face darkening, his eyes narrowed as Lukas closed his fist. He clocked the man sending him straight to the floor. Putting his boot on the man's chest, he said, "I wouldn't get up if I were you."

The Scot scrambled backward like a mouse who'd discovered the trap when Lukas removed his foot. "She's all yours."

Lukas stared down the opposite side of the room and took a stride forward. "Who else needs a reminder?"

Heads shook or men stared at the ceiling avoiding eye contact as soon as he looked at them. The instigators hid grins behind their drinks.

"Kindly take me home, Lukas." Juliana's soft voice came from very close behind him.

He turned around and took in the shambled remains of lace hanging off her torn blouse like rivulets of a weak, end-of-the-summer waterfall, and stained with his sticky red punch. Still modestly covered, but her outfit was as wholly ruined as her dripping hair. But it was the sad resignation in her expression that sucked the air out of his lungs.

No tears on her pale, punch-covered cheeks. She simply raised her chin and said in a resigned manner, "I think the point has been exceedingly well made."

He stepped back and allowed her to leave ahead of him, which she did with the dignity of a queen in the stark silence after the skirmish.

Lukas pulled a red kerchief out of his back pocket and handed it to her. "I'm very sorry."

She closed her eyes and made the smallest shake of her head. "I knew better than to come." Then she opened her eyes and dabbed at the already drying mess on her face and neck.

"Juliana—"

"Please. Let's just catch the next train."

"Yes."

Trains ran often to keep crews working, freight and supplies moving, twenty-four hours. At the least, they could find a spot on a platform out of the wind if there wasn't a passenger car. Her position afforded privileges with the Milwaukee Railroad. Under the circumstances, any one of the conductors would help her home the few miles between camps. But Lukas felt both the responsibility and the desire to see her all the way home.

"I suppose there's no saving this." She fluttered her hands in front of her body and then handed him back the soiled kerchief.

"No, I wouldn't think so." She had so little the damage must be dear. "But I'll replace it. You shouldn't spend the money you've worked so hard to save." He stuck his hands in his pockets.

"I can't replace what it meant to me, but thank you for the offer."

"Isn't it just a blouse? Surely—"

The lack of emotion in her face belied the intensity of her words. "This, Mr. Filips, is not just a blouse! I

had my first kiss and married my husband wearing it."
Pink crept into her cheeks, barely perceptible in the fast
coming dark. Mountain shadows had long since
blocked the setting sun, though the sky still held a
glow turning high, thin clouds peach and gold.

"I'm truly sorry for my part in destroying your
outfit." He hung his head. "My intention was to defend
your honor, not hurt and humiliate you."

"I know." She gave him her full attention, caramel
brown eyes sticking to his soul. "This was all my fault. I
knew better. But now you know why I keep to myself."
She touched the space of missing lace and loosely
hanging bodice. "Also, now you know why I'm grateful
you travel with me." She shivered. "What if that same
man had caught me alone? What if he'd been a merciless Montenegrin?"

"A what?" What did she have against Montenegrins?

"Never mind. I shouldn't have said that." She turned
away and watched the track for the train as if she could
will it to arrive faster.

"Please, Juliana, share why you feel Montenegrins
are merciless."

She remained quiet, only shaking her head, refusing
to speak further.

Someone had hurt her terribly. "There are good and
bad people everywhere, Juliana."

"And there are some I choose to avoid." She folded
her arms. "Press me further and you'll be one of them."

"Could you consider forgiving whatever happened?"
She gave him a glacial glare. "I'll see myself home."
He lifted his hands in surrender. "No. I'll not press."
She nodded as the train came through the tunnel.

"Thank you. Some things should be left alone and in the past."

How could he find out more if she wouldn't talk about it? Once they sidetracked and turned the train, Adair on Loop Creek would be two stops and a few minutes. He had a very short time to smooth over the strain between them.

"Will you bake tonight?"

"Once I clean up."

"Is there some way I can help ease the burden?"

"You want to help me bake? You know your way around a kitchen?" She arched a brow. "You really don't strike me as kitchen help."

"Well, I'm not such good help in the kitchen but I will do anything to make this day end better for you."

The stress on her face relaxed into bemusement. "In all this time, not one man has offered to help me other than get me to the train. And that has been because the station master requires it of the freightman in order to deliver the bread on time. The other bakers have husbands or, well, they have someone." She tipped her head as she thought about his offer. "Would you consider moving bags of flour for me while I clean up?"

"Juliana, I will do whatever you need."

Thank you, I accept your offer." The train slid into the East Portal stop. Juliana took a second glance at Lukas. "You know they weigh up to fifty pounds each, right?"

"Not as much as your handcart when it's full, yes?" He smiled. "I think I can manage."

She boarded the train and sat in the front row,

pulling her skirt aside so Lukas could join her on the bench of the very nearly empty passenger car.

Ah, progress. Without words, she'd invited him to take the place beside her that he'd wanted from the moment he'd caught sight of Juliana Hayes. But if she found out he was Montenegrin, would she really disassociate? Surely she'd know him well enough to overlook such a blanket prejudice. He sat, mulling over options. He had to get to the bottom of that prejudice.

Once at her cabin in Adair, she rewashed her sticky hair and changed, and he had already moved three large bags of flour from the storage shed to her work space. In the process, Lukas decided not to reveal his origins. At least not until Juliana and he grew closer.

For the rest of the time God graced him with the responsibility to protect her, Lukas would find a way to build her trust through acts of kindness. Then, he would tell her and overcome her bias because she would have his constant examples of goodwill. Then, he would win her heart as well. He needed to find out why she distrusted his people.

CHAPTER 6

EARLY AUGUST

"WHAT DO YOU KNOW ABOUT THE WIDOW Hayes?" Lukas asked Conductor Kelly while he waited for her to arrive at the platform.

He'd asked around where he dared the last few weeks, but no one seemed to know much about her. She kept to herself except to deliver the required bread rations and the disastrous dance. But the rides with her had been pleasant, the conversation kept to general topics. Lukas wanted to know her, truly know this woman. "How long has she been alone?"

"I ain't know'd her that long, sorry." He shrugged. "I been here 'bout a year. You could count it like dog years compared to most in this here valley." He laughed at his own joke. "She been widowed all that time, I figure. Weren't wearin' widow's weeds when I came." He looked at his watch, then in the direction of Juliana's cabin and brick ovens, and shook his head. "If'n she don't show up right quick, we gonna have to leave her to the next train." He shook his head again. "Hate to do it to a good woman. But I can't risk a pay cut. That ain't gonna bode well with the company if she misses the shift change."

"I'll see what's keeping her."

"Three minutes and I blow the whistle." He went to close a freight car door on his way to inspect for departure.

Lukas jumped off the train, jogged to the dirt path leading away from the platform to see down the direction she should be coming from.

She struggled with a handcart to push her load up the last small incline, brown skirt hem dragging in the rocks as she leaned hard into the steel handle.

Why wasn't anyone helping her? He ran the hundred yards to help. "Here, let me."

"The path is just rough here." But she sidestepped out of the way and used the apron corner to wipe her brow. The sun rose early and hot, getting hotter and the air drier by the hour.

"We have about two minutes to get you and your cargo aboard." He took off at a clip with her right behind.

"Karl, Simon, lend a hand!" He called out as he reached the front of the train. The two gave him less guff than the others as a general rule. He assumed it might have something to do with having wives. A woman settled a man. He glanced at Juliana. He wanted to be settled by her. Jonesy was right. He could get in line behind a couple hundred others vying for her attention. But none of them had daily access to build a relationship like he did.

The men jumped to the stairs at their foreman's command. Karl planted himself on the bottom step and Simon stood at the doorway.

Lukas hefted the first basket of ten fat, nourishing loaves to Karl. He passed it back to Simon, who passed it on to another, as the whistle blew for departure. The men moved the other baskets on board as Juliana shoved her cart out of the way.

Then the wheels budged and rolled forward until Lukas and Juliana had to run alongside.

Lukas seized the handle, swept an arm out and swung the surprised widow, brown skirt billowing like a sail, onto the step with him, pulling her in close to his body.

The train bumped heavily on the track heading into a turn. He instinctively pulled her tighter against his chest — purely to protect from the jostling train — but he had to fight the desire to lower his head and taste her lips. The little rusty flame sparking in her heated eyes tempted him so much he had to look away or he'd blow the plan he'd painstakingly thought through. She hadn't given him the chance to look that deeply into her eyes, not even when she'd begrudged him the dance just for show. He more than liked this perspective. With patience, his plan would open her heart. Act rashly, and he'd have as much chance as the hundreds she'd already rebuffed.

"You could have dropped me." Juliana's gaze slid past his shoulder and watched the track behind them fall away faster as she clutched his shirt. Her fingers tightened on the cloth.

"Never." He inhaled the scent of rose water, honey, and fresh bread that emanated from Juliana. The scent that clung so satisfying and welcoming to a man. The scent of home. "You will always be safe with me."

She pushed back with shaky hands when the train moved off the curve and onto a straight-a-way, but stopped at his words and whispered. "Until you aren't here just like—" She frowned dousing the fire in her eyes. "Never mind."

"I will be here for you." Lukas moved his arm away before she could push again, settling his hand in the small of her back to protect her from losing her balance as she climbed the last two steps.

She looked a bit rattled the way she stood instead of sitting. He didn't know whether from their acrobatics or that the baskets all ended up on the left bench so only one space for the two of them remained. Or could she be feeling a little like him, shaken from their closeness a moment ago?

"Way to go, Foreman! The next camp won't miss their grub."

"Shoulda been a trapeze artist." Rowdy joked, instigating laughter around him as he had instigated the Scot at the party.

"Already feels like a three-ring circus here to me with you clowns." Lukas shot back raising the level of laughter all the more, but this time redirected at Rowdy.

Karl clapped him on the shoulder. "Where's Harry

English and his camera? That'd a made the front page as downright heroic."

"Wouldn't have had a picture without you boys." He thanked Karl and Simon. "It's all in the teamwork." Then Lukas sat beside Juliana.

She scooted away as far as possible on the short bench without making it noticeable to those behind them and clasped her hands in her lap. With his size, she didn't have much room to move. But his closeness did something to her.

"That was good," she said not wanting to look him straight in the eyes. He might see how flustered he made her. "The way you build up your men."

"Always give credit where credit is due. My father taught me that. A man will give his best when it's appreciated." As he brushed the dirt from the cart and the train from his hands, he said, "Now tell me, please, why you had no help today."

Her chin turned slowly, until their eyes met. "You don't know?"

"I should know?"

Juliana looked confused. "You really don't?"

"I don't."

"Oh." She glanced away and then back at him. Not wanting the rest to hear, she leaned in toward his ear. "You remember Jacques? The baggageman working the Adair depot?"

"Yes?"

"He decided to take another job down the line as a firefighter. The pay is pretty good, I hear."

"Well that's not uncommon. The men move around as needed."

"I know, but now they can't fill this one at Falcon."

"Really?" He raised his brows. "Why?"

"The men are all afraid of you after, well, after the way you knocked out the brute at the dance. Jacques was there. After he'd pestered me for a date, he figured you'd come for him next. When the new jobs posted..." She shrugged, the rest understood.

"Ah, I see." He grinned. "So they don't want to be seen bothering you in order to avoid tangling with me."

She swallowed and looked away. "You're the problem. No one wants to come near me."

"I'm the problem? Seems I'm the solution. Unless you can make it to the departure on time, in addition to making sure you are safe on the train, I need to get you to the train."

She tucked a few strands of loose hair up into her scarf. "I don't know how you want to handle it. But I can't bake any faster than I already do. My workload is growing with the firefighters coming in for the spot fires."

He thought for a few minutes. "If you can be ready, the train is here long enough for me to get you and the cart up the path."

"I can be ready." She slumped against the seat seeming defeated. The largest publicly visible movement she'd made since they'd met. "I hate asking for help, but with so many loaves to deliver each day I can't do it myself."

She wasn't a small woman, reed thin with a waist as tiny as a wasp like the corseted socialites he'd met. Healthy and shapely, but small being relative to his size. She had strong arms and shoulders even for a woman of average height. With the physical demands of kneading so much dough, working the ingredients, and the other required duties living in these harsh mountains, Lukas admired Juliana's tenacity and strength — and the beauty of how that looked all put together along the length of her bare arms, thanks to the summer heat and her baking position. She wore short sleeves and calf-length skirts making it hard for him to look away. But a wooden handcart lined with steel meant for lighter trips in the mines, plus the load that overflowed the cart's bucket with each loaf weighing two pounds, landed a tad above the top of her abilities. Grown men felt the weight of that equipment.

"I'll come, before the start of my shift each day, for as long as you need me."

She looked up. "The company added Sundays to help with the fire crews. I'm to provide extra loaves each day of the week and a full order on Sunday as well. You realize that may be the rest of the summer."

His lips turned up slowly. "I hope so, Juliana. I told you I will be here for you."

She searched his face. "I believe you." She blushed. Then she added, "With the extra work, I might be able to leave sooner than I'd planned."

"Sooner?" His stomach coiled. Now what would he do?

"Yes," she glowed with anticipation. "Maybe as much as a few weeks."

He needed more time. As much time as possible before she left him to a cruel winter without her. Time to win her promise to wait for him wherever she planned to go.

"If this keeps up, and the fires stay way down the line, I'm thinking the first of September." Her eyes lit up with joy. "Won't that be wonderful? And you won't have to ride with me anymore."

How should he answer that? She didn't know the conductor told him he could ease up. A conversation Lukas requested be kept between the two men, earning him an elbow in the ribs from the older man. He'd said, "I'd keep that gal lassoed myself, if I was yous."

"I like our rides." He couldn't quite meet her eyes or she'd see the deep emotions stirring. "I hope you'll change your mind and stay. I'll miss you when you go, Juliana."

CHAPTER 7

Early morning
August 20, 1910

LUKAS TOOK THE WORN ENVELOPE FROM HIS
box at the Rowland Depot. For a moment, he couldn't
do more than stare at the handwriting. Not long, yet it
felt like ages since he'd stood on home soil. A year
working as a translator at Ellis Island, then he'd worked
his way west, always sending funds home to help
support the estate.

He jumped on board, greeting the conductor. "It's
going to be a good day, Kelly."

"Did ya see all those boys headin' home all week?
They're lettin' a few thousand off fire duty. Yep, gonna
be a good day."

He slid down, closed his eyes, and leaned his head
against the back of the uncomfortable seat for a

moment. He let his thoughts turn to Montenegro. He remembered what the manor looked like, the massive stone fireplace, and the velvet trappings around the windows pulled back to allow guests to walk in the gardens during parties. The way it looked when he was a child, full of people and the wonders of the world waiting for him.

Though he'd held off as much loss as he could, working the remains of the estate after his father's death, they needed to sell it before the economy crashed altogether. His sister would never get the promised dowry from the government. That infusion of Russian money, along with the rest, had long since disappeared, never making it past the prince's coffer to the people the donor had meant to support.

Prince Nikola continued taunting Russia with a teasing dalliance with Austria as a display of independence. The fine steps of his dance eroded the fortunes of the Filips family and many others over the years until many Montenegrins, like himself, struck out to find alternate means to support their families. If the prince wanted real independence, he'd learn how to manage the economy rather than living off other countries. He'd give teeth to the 1905 constitution so his people could prosper.

But now, with the blessings God poured out on him, his family could focus on building a life in America — without the land, deteriorating manor, and titles impoverishing them. A new life full of opportunity. He'd proven that as he took higher paying positions with each move.

In Montenegro, his title held him back in spite of

the higher education he'd been given. Here, all he had
to do was survive the coming cold, snowy winter and
he'd have enough to set up a home, and soon a school
for Montenegrin immigrants. So many here needed a
good international education. He could at least plan on
tutoring in the six languages he spoke.

His mother and sister could emigrate as soon as the
estate sold. He broke into a smile at the thought of
young men learning etiquette from the stern duchess
who'd often visited at court with her senate husband. If
he'd only had his mother to instruct his crews. The
vivid image brought a snicker. What would they think
of Idaho and Montana — and of the woman he loved?

Lukas sat up as the train pulled into Adair. Juliana
had her own plans. Would she consider altering them
to include him? Or would she be shamed by an abdi-
cating duke as a Montenegrin woman would?

Touching the letter in his breast pocket, he could
think of nothing better than to surround himself with
the love of family—and Juliana. With the fires dying
down, perhaps she wouldn't have to work Sundays
any longer. He'd ask her to spend her first Sunday off
with him, picnicking by a tributary away from prying
eyes. They could talk freely and plan the future
together. Away from the mines and rails, they could
build a life together. Away from here just as she
wanted.

Lukas greeted Juliana for their morning delivery ride
despite the growing summer storm. "Good morning."
Clouds overhead grew in thick, heavy formations trap-
ping in the remaining smoke from the dregs of distant
fires. The winds picked up, but no rain yet in the early

morning. "Looks like we're getting a break from the heat. Let's hope the rain comes with it."

Growing gusts buffeted dingy canvas shelters, snapping the tent flaps in the makeshift town, and creating a scene of rolling waves like whitecaps on the sea he'd sailed for freedom and fortune. He normally carried his coat and gear in a pack for deep mine supervision or pulling his weight on an undermanned shift, but today he might have to wear it.

"Morning," she said with happiness lighting her face. "I love the breeze. Last night when it started, I savored the cooler air. It pushed out all that stale smoke left over from those spot fires." She leaned in to tell her secret, smelling of rose water and the cinnamon she'd baked into the Sunday rolls. "I let my hair down and let it blow wild. It took me half an hour to comb it out."

How he wished he'd been there last night to see her hair stream out behind her, to run his hands through it. He'd been stuck indoors finishing his second round of monthly reports.

She laughed as she wrapped a thick brown shawl around her, overlapping it to tuck into her waistband. "It was worth it. We seem to be getting a little relief from the smoke," she glanced at the darkening clouds. "...and some moisture to break the drought by the looks of those." She gave a slight shiver. "But I'll be glad to be gone before winter sets in." A satisfied expression settled in her smile.

He pushed the thought of a winter without Juliana into the back of his mind. "That would be blessing indeed with how dry it's gotten around here. I know we've need them, but it's been hard to find enough seats for my crews since they've been sending so many fire fighters up and down the line. The pack horses take up space in the freight cars. I heard from Conductor Kelly this morning that they let quite a number go home now." He shared her elation. "Looks like the scare is over and the fires are mostly out."

"Couldn't be better news." She lifted a large picnic basket, hanging it over her elbow and balancing it on one hip. "All those extra batches has added to my savings, though I'm worn out. I haven't had a Sunday off the last three, even with all the bakers working extra shifts. The fire camps have needed five hundred loaves a day! I tell myself it means I can leave earlier. That helps keep me going."

"I hope there's a raisin cinnamon roll in there for me." He teased while pushing the load onto the path. But the aroma of sweet fruit and spice curled into his nostrils. "Otherwise my weakened muscles may give way under this load and the wind may very well blow me away."

She assessed his arms and shoulders as if at a military inspection, with a light of admiration in her eyes. "Tsk, tsk. We can't have you waste away, now can we?" She brought a large cinnamon bun out from under a tea towel. "Will this do?" Juliana pursed her lips to keep from breaking her straight face.

"Most definitely." He stopped and held out his hand to accept the edible gift. The cart had a mind of its own, rolling backward into his shin. "Ow, ow, ow..." he hopped backward as he grabbed at the handle to halt building momentum. His pride felt the smash more deeply than his leg.

She pressed one hand against her mouth holding back the mirth. "I'm sorry. Really." But as she spoke, a giggle burst out. "I hope that won't spoil your day." A gust blew her skirts against her legs, outlining her slender, athletic form. "I'll just carry this to the train for you."

Drawn to the sparkle in her eyes, Lukas spit out the first thing he could think of before he risked all he'd been working toward by snatching her up and kissing her. "I have a letter from home."

"How wonderful!" She beamed joy through his soul with her beautiful smile as if the common eagles overhead lifted him up on the drafts where they hung suspended. "Did you get good news?"

"I haven't read it yet."

"How could you not?"

"I'd have been late getting to you."

Her cheeks blossomed rosy red. Would she consider a real relationship with him in the future if she knew not only his origins, but his family obligation? Surely every woman wanted to marry well. In America, titles didn't seem to matter. Only the ability to provide a future held importance. Her dream of a bakery could blend perfectly with his dream of a school. She might want to take students to learn the trade as assistants. He could taste the possibilities as surely as he would that cinnamon bun she held.

Once on board, and Juliana settled with her wares stowed, Lukas looked to the oncoming storm. He and most of the other passengers, closed their windows against the strengthening wind. "It's really picking up out there." He sat down and accepted the roll made just for him.

Juliana patted his arm. "Go ahead now. If I had a letter from home, I couldn't wait to open it."

After he finished eating, and praising her skills, Lukas pulled out the letter and read in silence, savoring the news. He shared a surprise tidbit. "My mother and sister will come soon." His smile grew with each line. The estate had a potential buyer, an Italian.

She turned from watching out the window. "They will? That's wonderful!" Juliana looked at the letter and envelope in his hands.

"There are rumors the prince will proclaim himself king."

"A king. They're overseas then?" She pointed at the postmark. "I haven't seen one like that."

He realized too late his folly of sharing the letter. America didn't have a prince and he was from the one place Juliana couldn't tolerate. "I've been sending money to help with expenses."

"Lukas, where is home?" She waited with patience, but a patience that wouldn't be distracted this time.

Had the time spent together built enough trust for what she asked now? He steeled himself. "Juliana, do you trust me?

"Why would you ask that? You've given me no reason to distrust you."

He swallowed. "Because my homeland is Montenegro."

Her eyes opened wide as she pushed her back against the corner of the seat, near the window. "Montenegro." She looked away as if the regular movement onto the sidetrack making room for the eastbound held a special fascination. "You tell me this now and you ask me for trust?"

"I hoped you'd see that where I'm from doesn't determine our friendship or our future. We are two people with all we can imagine in front of us."

But even as he spoke, he saw the wall rebuilt between them in the space of seconds as she retreated with a coldness behind it. "Where you're from..." She said in her quiet, too calm way. "Yes, it matters very much where you're from to me."

He kept his voice down as well. He'd prefer this conversation in private, but a niggling doubt warned him it wouldn't happen. Best not to let it fester. Or give her a chance to sneak away unknown. For all he knew, she'd met her goal already. "At least tell me why you feel so strongly. I feel I've earned that much. Do we not share a mutual respect?"

She sized him up much like she did when they first met. Her eyes held pain though, not aloof anger. This time, those eyes planted grief in his heart. Grief because he saw her pull away. Grief at the loss he felt coming. The root of grief might prove more dangerous to his heart. He could not allow it to take root.

"My husband died because he broke up a fight between Montenegrins, and one died in the process. It was a horrible accident, but not his fault. Hayes didn't start it. His job was to keep men working, keep them alive, not get murdered because Montenegrins can't behave like civilized people."

Voices rose behind them, as if on cue. She turned to

see, then gave him a pointed look. With a small huff, she continued, "They fight with Italians. They fight with Serbians. They fight with one another. Is there anyone a Montenegrin won't fight?" She paused scalding him with judgement. Without waiting for his response, she added, "I think not."

"How many were in that fight, Juliana? The entire country? How is it you don't feel that way about the Scotch? Remember it was a Scot that assaulted you at the dance and a Montenegrin, me, that stopped it."

"You've conveniently forgotten it was Rowdy and his Montenegrin gang that set the Scot up. Who really bore the responsibility?"

"I've been here all summer working with men from all around the world. Of the seventy plus different nationalities, I have at least six under my command including Montenegrins, Italians, Croatians — sometimes more. I haven't had nearly the trouble foremen in the past have had even with the constant rotation. Is it possible leadership is the issue and not one group of people?"

He'd gone too far from the stricken, white parlor of her cheeks.

"Now you're casting aspersion on my husband's character and leadership?"

"No, Juliana. No." He reached out toward her.

She pushed herself against the window.

"Truly, that's not my intention. What if you could determine there were ten good Montenegrins like those who have helped you on and off the train? Or those who are grateful for the food you provide?" Lukas caught her stormy gaze. "What if there were one? Me."

He caught her hand. "That's why I didn't tell you. I wanted a chance to prove to you through serving. Serving your needs has been an honor. You've met my men. Simon and Karl helped you just this morning."

Confusion lightened her features from the betrayal. "I'd say you were trying to get around what I know. You ordered them to help."

"But they did help. Would you condemn them all for a few?"

"Reality is reality. I condemn no one."

"Don't you? Don't you condemn me now?" He lifted her hand to his heart. "See me. I'm more than where I was born. I'm the man who—"

"Lied by omission." Juliana tugged her hand away. "I would have trusted you, but then you intentionally deceived me for weeks. Am I wrong? Or did you purposefully withhold who you really are?" She stood as the train came to a stop.

How could he get through to her? "I will do this as I have without fail." Lukas took hold of the bread bin handles. "I have not changed, Juliana, simply because you know where I was born." What would happen if she knew of his nobility? His heart pounded like the drums during the royal parades.

Her eyes clouded, but she turned without a word. Then she stopped at the top stair and looked back. "You have helped me beyond what should have been expected." She cleared her throat. "I know that."

Thank you, Lord! She was softening, beginning to come around.

Conductor Kelly met them on the Falcon platform, yelling over the howling wind. "Just got given a telegraph fer ya, Foreman. Sounds like ya got a situation back there in Rowland." A streak of lightening cracked across the sky followed by an intense boom echoing through the valley. The wind kicked up as if it'd absorbed the energy between Lukas and Juliana.

With the delivery basket in his arms, Lukas raised his voice above the wind, "What's it say?" He tipped his head in the direction of the depot to get them all out of the storm. "Tell me inside."

Lukas set the crate near the area Juliana unloaded each morning, filling several bunkhouse baskets. They'd be picked up by the various cooks in Falcon at the end of each shift to round out the crew meals.

The conductor continued, "You're down two men on the morning shift up at Rowland. Been a scrape 'tween yer night and day crews."

Juliana stood and turned around, her face bland as her words. "So there's been another fight."

"Yep, a big one sounds like."

Lukas could hear the death knoll on their relationship. He tried to end the conversation. "I'll get on it. Thank you."

Picking up a freight list from the communication board, the conductor added, "Gotta give it to 'em, they're a tough bunch. You been keepin' it better controlled than we seen in the last three, four years."

Juliana's face darkened at the conductor's innocent declaration.

A sprinkle, more like a spit or two, darkened the wood outside the door as he opened it to head back to the train. "Maybe the rain will help. This heats been makin' things worse. Only so much any man can take."

He nodded, acknowledging the praise while his hope deflated. The squeeze in his chest built at the thunder in Juliana's eyes.

Lukas set the crate on the floor, running a hand across the back of his neck. Sure, he'd had a few skirmishes over the summer. The job, conditions, and temperaments that came with this kind of back-breaking monotony had occasional pressure releases. But that didn't speak for his people, only the situation. She had to see the unforgiveness she held onto was unreasonable.

But this situation with his men had to be handled or it would escalate. "I'm sorry, Juliana, I have to go back and take care of this. But we'll finish our talk when I get back."

"No, I think we're done."

"Juliana—"

"You need to go." She picked up her empty basket and walked past him. The wind whipped at her shawl and skirt as she boarded the train on the sidetrack headed to Kyle and Stetson.

The lightning and thunder picked up their efforts, creating a massive show in the heavens. He blew out a heavy sigh. At least God knew how he felt.

Lukas climbed the stairs on the eastbound. *Lord, please grant me the chance to make this right.*

CHAPTER 8

Juliana startled at the double crack of thunder as lightening flashed close enough to reverberate through the tracks. She pressed her cheek against the window to see if the strike left smoking woodland nearby. But crane as she might, she couldn't find the spot from her seat in the speeding train. Lightning mixed with the high winds were not a good combination. They needed a deluge to get the forest good and soaked.

The conductor came on board. "Sorry, folks, schedule change means everybody off." A groan ran through the car. "We gotta head down the valley and pick up folks at Avery. They got a wildfire startin'. Everybody off."

Grouchy and grumbling workers, who'd been breathing smoke from surrounding fires for weeks except when underground in cold, damp conditions, stumbled and shuffled off the train. Their frustrated fatigue evident. This night crew wouldn't get back to their bunks for a while.

Juliana caught the conductor's attention. "Mr. Kelly, I have to make the deliveries to the camps." She pointed to the hundred loaves, more than double her normal quota since they'd added the fire camps. She'd been contemplating hiring a boy to deliver if this volume kept up. But if fire fighters were heading home, she couldn't spare the funds. "Can't I stay?"

"Sorry, Mrs. Hayes, we don't got the time for the extra stops. See the smoke comin' up down yonder?" He pointed at a distant dark plume that thickened as they spoke. "They got a bunch of lightning strikes south of Avery today. We got a telegraph sayin' they're closin' the tracks except fer firefighters after this here train. The wind is winnin' down at St. Joe City and the fire looks to be headin' this way into the valley."

They needed every seat. "I understand." She shivered, whether at the unexpected chill from the overcast skies, or fear, Juliana couldn't tell. "What about all that bread?"

"Since we ain't stoppin', just leave the bread. If the fire stays back, I'll get the baggageman at Stetson and Kyle depots to help unload on the way back. We'll pick you up once we got the folks at Avery out of danger. But we ain't takin' anybody closer to it." He leaned out the door keeping an eye on his work. "Best bet's gonna be an hour or two. We'll lay her out and make it a quick trip. Might as well get a good meal down ya. I think they're gonna work ya to the bone after this." He poked a thumb down the track. "Think them boys they let go will be comin' back."

"Let's hope they're not needed." Juliana smiled at him as she took the steps down toward the platform. She turned back. "Just come back safe, Mr. Kelly. What you're doing is heroic. I'll keep you all in my prayers." She waved at his salute as the train pulled out.

Hot food hadn't held any interest most of the summer. She ate to keep up her strength. But with the cooler day, she took the conductor's advice and headed over to the Falcon dining room while lightning and thunder flashed and boomed down the valley. She focused on her meal to keep her mind off the howling winds, increasing lightning strikes – and the threat.

Strong gusts weren't unusual through the winding valley. Often coming one direction in the morning and changing in the evening. This, though, was somehow a different kind of blast carrying heat from miles away ending the mild cooling with a suffocating pall.

CHAPTER 9

Lukas arrived at Roland, three long whistles alerting the town and depot workers. The telegraph operator ran to the engine waving a sheet of paper the wind tried to yank away. "Johnnie, you gotta go back now!"

The engineer, Johnnie Mackedon, shouted out of his window, "What's wrong?"

"They're shutting down all the mines and log camps. The fire converged and blew up at Avery." The operator climbed up far enough to hand off the full message.

Lukas jumped off the steps and ran toward the railroaders to better hear the emergency. He had men in camps all along the line—and Juliana, where was she? Had she gone down past Stetson to Avery or did she get warned in time and stay in Falcon?

"Johnny, what's the plan?"

"We got word that the wind has fanned embers into a massive fire back southwest of Avery." He never stopped working as he shot off the rest. "Hurricane force winds blasted through St. Joe City into the back country. A wall of fire is headed this way."

"What do you need me to do?" Lukas shouted over the building howl.

"Get the passengers off and unhitch those full freight cars. Let's turn her around and get as many out of there as possible!"

The telegraph operator shouted more information. "There should be slew heading up toward Falcon. The tracks closed about thirty minutes ago downline from there."

Lukas grabbed the man's arm, holding him back before he jumped down. "Send a message. Send it as fast as you can. Tell everyone to get to the depot platform. We'll get them from there."

Panic bit his belly spreading the poison of terror. Terror for all the people he knew, but especially for Juliana.

"Johnnie, I'm with you! The Angel of Adair is down there."

The engineer sized him up in a second. He agreed by pointing Lukas to the coupling. It'd become too difficult to talk over the din.

Lukas signaled back he understood. Adrenaline poured into his bloodstream as Lukas raced to assist.

He bounded on the first car as they put all the full freight cars in the hole on the side track. With the forest service out of the threatened area this last week, Juliana's regular delivery, from Adair to the small camp town of Falcon, took a deadly turn. Could he find her and get his men out before the wall of fire overtook them?

Johnnie leaned out the window and yelled, "Aboard or not, we're pulling out!" He pulled several short whistles—signaling emergency—and set the train on its rescue mission.

Lukas clung on the side. He scrapped in behind the fuel load as the smoke darkened, growing heavier as they careened down the track at the maximum speed Johnny could command. Coughing, Lukas tied his kerchief over his face. The hot winds slammed into them, slowing the progress of the powerful engine. *Lord be with us, we're riding into the beast.*

They passed Adair in record time, Johnnie laying on the whistle sounding the emergency.

CHAPTER 10

An hour in, everyone waited for the train in the village dining hall. People jammed in around the tables, and all available space, with nowhere else to go in the storm. Then the hurricane winds hit Falcon. The wooden dining hall creaked and swayed under the onslaught. Noise so loud people ducked, covered their ears, and cringed in fear as the trees bending and breaking around them reverberated through the electrified air. Some scrambled under the tables.

"Fire!"

She had no idea who yelled out the warning, but Juliana rose in the ensuing panic and fought to get to the door. As soon as the first person swung it wide, the door ripped off its hinges and flung outward into the storm. Sparks and ash fell like a fine mist. The canvas over the dining area would surely be next!

A cook ran in from the stoves. "Help! My babies are in the school. My babies!"

Every man snapped into action. Children were the one thing all agreed must be protected. Hardened miners could be found playing peek-a-boo with a baby or tossing a ball back to a boy. No one wanted harm to come to a little one. Juliana begrudgingly admitted the one redeeming factor for those she had no reason to respect otherwise from their treatment of her.

An off-duty mine foreman, took charge. "Crew Three, get the kids out of the school! Crew Four, go through the town and look for stragglers. Tell 'em all to get to the depot."

The lead called back, "None o' those kids weighs much. They're so little the wind will blow them away!"

"Tie 'em to you then. Whatever you have to do, but get the kids to the depot. Their folks can meet them there." He bellowed out, "Move!"

The crews that had been groggily waiting to get to their bunks shot forth with grim determination etched into grayed faces.

In less than fifteen minutes the entire town and unexpected guests, over a hundred men, women, and children banded together on the Falcon platform straining to hear a train whistle over the roaring winds. Little ones cried and clung to any safe adult. Townspeople and mining crews circled the children with linked arms against the wind. A few miners had belted the smallest children to their legs like odd three-legged competitors.

Trees exploded sending fireballs into the sky like Roman rockets as the fire devoured the canyon. The crowd's screams lost in the volume as a tornado of fire and wind whipped up heading right for Falcon. The roar louder than ten freight trains at full speed.

Juliana's scream ripped out of her throat, stolen, as the spinning monster took out a line of trees at the edge of town. The dining hall went up in flames along with the school and several bunkhouses. There wasn't anything left to block the view of the storm leveling the small town building by building. The heat radiated like a giant oven drying rain before it could hit the decking.

The smoke thickened until everyone coughed, eyes watered, and rivulets of ash mixed with tears trickled down cheeks. Massive chunks of burning wood landed all around them. She kicked at them to send them into the dirt like she saw the others doing. The roof on the depot caught and flamed one log after another like a candelabra. The smoke and ash forced her to cover her mouth and nose, breathing through her shawl in sips of searing air.

The train was nearly on top of the stop before anyone at Falcon could hear or see it through the smoke. Flames licked at the dry, wood platform as the engine backed onto the sidetrack. The crowd ran for it only to discover no cars.

Engineer Johnnie Mackedon leapt from the front shouting to someone to help hook up the empty logging flatbed.

A shadow moved through the smoke, assisting, then disappeared to appear again on the platform. "Let's go! Get on and get your heads down!" He yelled through a wet, red kerchief tied to cover his nose and mouth. "Juliana! Juliana, are you here? Ju-li-an-a!"

She vaguely heard her name over the gale. Lukas? She ran to him. "Lukas!"

He threw his arms around her, shouting over the cacophony. "I'm here. Let's go!"

The entire crowd clambered off the burning railway platform onto the flatcar like a flock of crows landing on a carcass.

Juliana helped him hand children up to outstretched arms. When all were aboard, Lukas lifted Juliana and then jumped up after her.

"Down! Everyone lie down!" He pushed as many on their bellies as he could reach, motioning for them to do the same all the way up the flatbed as Johnnie rolled the train out of the station heading for safety.

Juliana lay on the very edge, mere inches to spare. Lukas covered her body with his holding tight to the side as the car swayed back and forth, buffeting in the sixty-plus mile an hour winds. As far as she could tell, they'd saved everyone from Falcon.

But the wall of flames licked up the mountainsides like a hungry, crazed dog coming after them attacking with a ferocity through thick undergrowth and trees so dry from the drought the furnace could rival Hades.

Johnnie seemed to be gaining ground as they approached Tunnel 28.

The hurricane winds battered the passengers with debris. Tree branches, falling trunks, pieces of tent material flew into the crowd. As fast as they could, burning hands in the process, they threw pieces off the train and off one another.

A chunk of burning wood landed on Juliana's skirt. Lukas lifted up on his elbow and kicked it off her, keeping it from burning through the material as the engine chugged into the tunnel.

Water dripping from the tunnel ceiling wet the clothing of all exposed. The tunnel hadn't yet lost its cold, fresh air to the vortex sucking the life out of everything in its path. For a few moments, Juliana and Lukas gulped in oxygen with the rest of the terrified escapees.

The hot mega gust hit them coming out the other side as the train raced uphill to the trestle ahead. It crossed a tributary into Loop Creek. They had to pass over before the fire burned the bridge out.

Another gust blasted into them. Lukas lost his grip. In a tangle of skirts, Juliana and Lukas flew off the end of the flatcar into the underbrush. Her scream echoed back from the mouth of the tunnel they'd just exited like the screech of a mockingbird.

CHAPTER 11

THOUGH THE UNBURNED BRANCHES
protected them from broken bones, Juliana's face and
neck felt scraped and bloodied from the dry, sharp pine
needles. Her scarf had blown off somewhere in the fall.
She had nothing to keep the smoke from her lungs or
her hair out of her face.

"Can you run?" Lukas grabbed for her hand.

She saw the smoke puffing through the tunnel like
an awakened dragon of old. The fire would be on them
in no time. "Yes."

"We have to go down," he pointed to the water
below. "Tie up your skirt, run to the trestle and start
climbing down."

Her eyes went wide as she traced the trestle's beams
and bars. "That's more than a hundred feet." She
coughed. "I don't think I can."

"Either you do or you don't trust me." He took her
face between his hands and made her focus on him.
"I'll go first. I'll be with you the whole way. Just slide

down each one and I'll catch you before we go to the next."

She nodded, tears pouring down her cheeks, drying before hitting her chin. Her long hair whipped all around them. Blinded, she caught as much as she could and wrapped it into her neckline.

"We go to there," he pointed over the edge to the earthen bank. "Not so far, right?"

She nodded she understood. Not the whole way down.

"Once over the edge, move in the direction of the bank. We can work our way down to the water hanging onto the bushes and trees."

The roar of the fire grew closer drowning out his last words. Fireballs sailed overhead like comets as the train shrank into the distance.

"What?"

"Now!"

Juliana grabbed his outstretched hand and ran to the edge of the trestle. She yanked the bottom of her skirt through her legs and jammed it into her waistband creating wide trousers. Then after tying the shawl around her waist, she followed Lukas onto the first rung. Sliding her foot until she felt his hand on her ankle, he steadied her descent. Her low-heeled boots helped by acting as a hook to find the next foothold. Her hands were strong from two years of kneading dough. But that didn't help the fact that she hung far above the river rocks shaking in terror. Her hip-length hair dislodged, flowing out like a cape, and blocked her view of Lukas. She froze in place.

"Faster, Juliana! We have to get in the water!"

The air sucked up, up into the demon above pulling all her hair upward, twisting toward the sky.

Lukas motioned to her to start moving toward the side where the trestle met the built up earthen foundation.

Her arms felt the strain and the insteps of her feet would bear the bruises for days, if they survived.

The fire laced fingers across the top of the tunnel, cresting the mountain, as they neared the valley bottom. Juliana's foot missed a rail and her arms gave out. She slid, smacking her chin on the next bar and rattling her teeth, until she landed in the circle of Lukas' arms where he clung to the trestle a yard below, hair pooling around her shoulders.

"I've got you." He soothed her as the fire leapt onto the trestle above. "Let's go, three more rails." They crawled down together to see flames curling down the hillside in front of Tunnel 28, as if blown by the devil dragon himself.

Lukas picked Juliana up and ran for the water. He jumped in feet first splashing Juliana into the shallow stream onto her side. Then he rolled her to completely soak her clothing and hair. She came up sputtering as Lukas dove down doing the same to himself.

He was up in a split second, hauling her up from the unnaturally warm water with him. "Now we run! Stay in the creek. We can keep dunking ourselves until we find safety."

"How? How do we get to safety?" She yelled over the cacophony. Had any sound come from her?

"We'll follow the creek north to the next train station we can find. If we hurry, we might catch them at Moss Creek. They still have to pull uphill through Adair. That switchback takes long enough we can get to them using the logging road, as long as it's clear."

They fought through the rocky stream stumbling and coughing with the fire chasing their heels like a hound scented on a fox. The animals, though, had already run for higher ground.

Juliana fell for what must be the umpteenth time. Knees bruised and hands bleeding, Lukas wouldn't let her stay down except to soak her clothing again and again, the heat drying them too quickly. "My shawl is wool, Lukas. I can't keep going with the weight of it if you keep getting it wet, too."

"You have to keep it. That may mean life and death if the smoke gets so thick again." He dipped it into the stream, wiped her face to clear the smoke and ash from her eyes, then tied it around his own waist. "I'll carry it for you."

She nodded and took his hand.

Three hundred yards more and they crossed onto the logging road. They ran as hard as they could into the clearing leading to Moss Creek, lungs clamoring for clean air. They didn't have to go all the way to know they were too late.

Everyone was long gone—or dead. The fire sizzled away the canvas, structure beams collapsed burning like stacked campfires. No more trains were coming up the track through the wall of fire that chased them, consuming every ounce of life in its way. Any train behind them no longer existed. Juliana prayed the one they'd been on made it through.

"We cannot stop." He grabbed her elbow and turned

them due north, away from the fire rushing in from the south and toward the mountains ahead still unmarred by the dragon's breath behind them.

The smoke, thick as heavy fog, clogged Juliana's lungs as she tried to keep pace with Lukas' long legs. She pressed the heel of her hand against her side.

He noticed, looked behind them, and scooped his arm around her propelling her forward. "Keep moving."

"If the fire doesn't get us, I think my heart will give out." She doubled over, hacking and wheezing as ash snowed all around, cinders setting off dry brush wherever it landed.

"Juliana," Lukas stooped down and pulled the red kerchief off his face, close enough to shout over the storm and see her eyes. "You are my heart. If yours stops then mine does. I will not let that happen." He brought her knuckles to his lips.

"I can't keep going." She wheezed out word by word.

"I'm not moving without you. So if we stay, it's your choice. This is your chance to get retribution on a Montenegrin." He took his hands away. "I surrender. Is that what you want?"

Flaming projectiles soared overhead. She screamed, "No! I want you to live!"

"Good!" He grinned infusing her with his optimism though his face was covered in dirt and soot. "I have plans for our future and I think God gave them to me." His chest heaved as he breathed, hands on his knees. "Do you at least believe in God?"

She doubled over again dragging in deep rasping breaths, arm wrapped around her torso against the sharp spasms. She saw the resolve in his eyes, and nodded.

Lukas ripped off an already torn sleeve, pressed it against the damp shawl at his waist, and then tied it around Juliana's nose and mouth. "Look up there."

She searched the area, following where he pointed. A round opening in the swell of rocks on the mountain. A tunnel! Cool, fresh air!

"Let's go."

She straightened her shoulders. God had sent this man into her life to give her courage for this trial. She would trust God and trust the gift of a heroic man. If she should perish, at least she gave her all as he did for her. Juliana held out her hand this time. "Lead on."

CHAPTER 12

HALFWAY UP THE MOUNTAIN, LUKAS GUIDED Juliana into the mouth of the tunnel. The beams held up boulders above the entrance. The tunnel had been blasted out of sheer rock. But the outside light reached a back wall. The air was already warming, though still fresh. For how long? The valley below would be engulfed soon.

"Take a short rest, Juliana." He removed their kerchiefs. "Then we have to head out."

"What?" She leaned over to see the pack mule path they'd just clambered up. The fire below wouldn't have fuel up close to the boulders around the abandoned tunnel. "We should be safe here, shouldn't we?" She stumbled toward the inner sanctum, leaning heavily on the wall. The sweet air relieved the burning pressure in her chest.

Lukas bent over, both hands on his knees this time, and sucked in oxygen. He shook his head. "Not enough room in here to shelter us when it hits."

As she recovered a bit from the run, Juliana knew he could make it out if it weren't for her slowing him down. "Why did you come?"

"What do you mean?"

"You're educated, have manners, and can do just about anything. Why here? Why this forsaken piece of wilderness?"

"Because I have family and responsibilities that require support."

"So this isn't about getting rich quick for you like so many others?"

"No. It's about helping my people." He cocked his head, listening. "Do you hear that? I think there could be clean water in here."

Lukas lifted a hand feeling along the rock walls for weeping, moving deeper into the tunnel. "Why didn't you go back to your family after your husband died?"

She pressed her hands to the rock on the other side of the narrow shaft. "My father told me that if I married Hayes, I should not come back."

"That seems harsh. He didn't approve of your marriage?"

"No. When I wrote home to tell them I was widowed because he was murdered by a Montenegrin, my mother wrote back that my father had died of a heart ailment."

"So those men deprived you of your husband and the further cruelty of finding out your father died left you without options."

Her voice cracked. "I'd broken his heart and I'll never see him again." She took another breath of air, though it seemed not as cool as before. "Then my mother said she was going home to Helena, Montana and I should follow her there."

"So you are going home." He moved his hand back to squeeze her fingers. "I understand. That's a good choice."

"I was. We sent letters back and forth, communicating again. I was so happy." She turned her hand palm up and held his needing human contact. "My mother died last summer of the flu. I couldn't get to her in time."

"You're an orphan and a widow. You've been doing this all alone." He took two strides, pulling her to him and holding her tight. "I'm so sorry."

Her cheek pressed to his chest, she nodded though the scrapes stung against his rough shirt. "I still have an aunt and uncle there. But they can't support me."

In the hazy light, Juliana tipped her head back, searching his eyes. "Those men stole everything right down to my future."

"You know none of those men were on my crews, don't you?"

She nodded. "The sheriff arrested the man who did it almost immediately." Her lungs ached, but the anger and unforgiveness pressed harder on her soul. "I don't want to hate anyone anymore."

His palm caressed her soot-covered cheek as his lips touched hers, stinging and chapped and yet electricity sang through her veins. She found herself as thirsty for his love as for water — and that shot panic through her body. She stepped back, feeling for the chiseled rock. Her fingers slid into a crevice, water trickled over them. "I found it!"

Spinning around Juliana cupped her hands, pointing her fingertips into the fissure, funneling the cold water to her mouth. It ran pure, almost freezing her throat as it spilled down her bodice. Pulling away, she invited Lukas to share. "It's sweet and so good."

He did the same, taking turns with her until they had enough.

"Juliana, we have to go. The smoke is getting heavier outside the tunnel." He pointed toward the front at wisps that widened as they watched. "And the air inside is getting hotter. Soon it's not going to be safe as the fire feeds on the air from this shaft. It will suffocate us. Get as wet as you can."

He knelt and splashed at the mud puddle on the ground while she pressed her body into the running rivulets. Then he took his kerchief, the makeshift kerchief from his sleeve, and her shawl wetting them as best he could.

"When we get out of this, you're marrying me."

"No," She shook her head. "I've saved for two years. I'm opening my pastry shop in Helena."

He folded her back into his arms. "It's all gone by now, Juliana, all gone."

The money she'd saved, everything destroyed. Her dream up in flames. "I'm lost then. I have no future again."

"You have me, and you are my heart. We can rebuild our lives together." He leaned down and kissed her. "Say you'll marry me. Give me the hope to get us out of here alive."

They'd never make it. Smoke already billowed into the cave. "I'll marry you, if we get out of here alive."

"A Montenegrin?"

"You have proven to me that a good man is a good man." Hope sprang up in her at the joy in his face. She'd make good on that promise—if they survived.

He grinned, white teeth almost glowing against his dirty, soot-covered face. "God is not finished with us. If you will not trust me to save your life, then trust God. He put us on this journey toward each other. He's not going to let it end like this. Yes?"

"Yes."

Lukas tied their kerchiefs on. Then he put his arm around her again and let her lean into him as they moved into the path of the fire.

Smoking mountains, blackened forests, and a rolling cloud of smoke encroaching as the blaze flattened and scorched all creation.

For a moment, neither could move at the sight of hell on earth coming to swallow them up. For Juliana, hope exploded like the massive cedars sending shreds of bark sparking high into the sky. Then she felt Lukas yank her from the ridge.

They slid and rolled down to a creek, smaller than the last, that flowed toward them. "That means we're heading toward Wallace, Idaho." As the haze shifted, Lukas and Juliana dunked as best they could.

"Don't drink that." He blocked her as she cupped her hands. "It's full of the fallout and getting too warm." Lukas' eyes grew enormous as his gaze lifted past her. "We've got to move." He pointed at the fire spreading into the trees about to circle their location. "There, head up again!"

Juliana's thigh muscles burned and her calves felt

like hot, pulled taffy but she kept moving. Lukas stayed behind her and splayed his hands around her hips giving her momentum until the hill flattened out into a mule trail. Then her legs gave out. She hit the ground, rocks biting into her skin.

Lukas slipped his arms around her and lifted. "Arms around my neck. Press in as close as possible. I need your weight as close to center to help me."

She squeezed tightly to his shoulders and whispered, "I'm so sorry. I have nothing left."

"We're going to make it." He took off following the trail. "There has to be a longer mine around here. You say the prayers. That's going to keep us going."

She obeyed, closed her eyes, and prayed with her head tucked into his neck, her mouth just below his ear. "Lord, see us. Help us. Strengthen Lukas and guide us to safety." She jerkily repeated the same words over and over as he stumbled through the rough terrain. She tried not to cry out when he tripped and dropped them both to the ground.

Visibility lowered to a few yards. If Lukas couldn't see, they'd likely run off a cliff.

"A horse!" Lukas rasped. "I see a horse and someone on it!"

She turned her face forward. A long line of men with picks and shovels shuffled ahead on the mountain trail. Firefighters!

By the time Lukas caught up to where they'd been, they'd disappeared.

"In here!" A voice called.

Lukas spun in the direction of the thin sound finally finding a man looking down from the mouth of a dark tunnel. "Juliana, look! If I put you down, can you climb up that outcrop?"

He'd been carrying her. She could crawl up a bunch of rocks. "Yes."

The voice called again, "Go back ten feet and come up there."

A steep, overgrown trail tramped down by men and horses led right to the mine shaft. Lukas set Juliana ahead of him. They half crawled, half climbed the couple of yards to the six-by-ten opening surrounded by overgrown shrubs. Both collapsed from exhaustion.

An inch or so taller than Lukas, a man leaned down and picked up Juliana from her knees. "Glad to see more alive. Let's see if we can keep it that way."

Lukas nodded, but couldn't stop coughing.

"Ed Pulaski. This here's my fire crew." Ed motioned him farther back. "Catch your breath and get your woman to the back where she'll be safest." He turned to his men. "Get me an axe. We gotta get these shrubs outta here!"

The tunnel ended in another dead-end, but it was at least a hundred yards deep before it'd been abandoned. Heavy beams reinforced the ceiling here, too. A few lanterns illuminated two horses and men strewn all over the floor. A small puddle here and there, but not much weeping water as in the last mine.

"Will we have enough air?" Juliana asked as tendrils of smoke snaked into view at the cave mouth. Soon the black smog would follow and choke them all.

"I don't know." He brushed her hair with his lips. "But it's the best chance we have. The fire's coming on too fast."

At the entrance, Ed Pulaski formed a sort of bucket brigade. "Get any blankets you have out of your packs. Find the puddles and soak them. We gotta cover these posts and this exit. Find me some nails!"

Men scrambled into action. While they worked, Juliana searched the saddlebags for canteens. Finding one, she found a slow drip high on the wall and held the canteen under it.

"Who has any tent pegs? Or horseshoe nails?"

Men produced anything they could find. Lukas grabbed an axe and helped pound tent spikes to anchor the makeshift door into the walls at Ed Pulaski's instructions. "If that wood burns, we're in trouble." He turned to everyone. "Fill your hats with as much water as you can get and keep these things wet."

With no hat or helmet, Lukas and Juliana turned to the injured men leaning against the tunnel walls. Lukas borrowed another canteen, dry as a bone, and started filling his while Juliana helped a downed man sip out of hers. Then they'd switch vessels for filling.

The fire raged, sucking under the blanket at the clean oxygen and singeing the blankets. Steam floated off the wool leaving dry patches.

"No!" Ed yelled as he fought singed material. He called for more water, holding the edges tight. "Get down low and stay down. The lower you are, the more likely you'll survive!"

One of his men panicked and ran like he'd tear his way out.

Juliana screamed at the sudden panic hitting the men around her.

The horses tried to rear and break for the entrance,

but Lukas grabbed one and a firefighter snagged another.

Ed had his revolver pointed at the terrified man who'd started the trouble. "You try it and I'll shoot you down."

He backed away. "We're gonna die in here."

"We're going to live." He kept his gun up, slowly aiming around the cavern. "I'm getting home to my family, and so are you."

Juliana could plainly see the blisters and burn marks on his hands. His sleeves were blackened to his shoulders, moustache and eyebrows nearly gone.

"The next man who tries to leave the tunnel, I'll shoot." He stared them all down the way Lucas did his miners on the train. "The only job you have is to get water up here to keep this all wet."

He stood there, guarding the door the rest of the night as the mountains roared like a thousand freight trains behind him, as far as Juliana could tell—until she passed out...

CHAPTER 13

Early morning
   August 21, 1910

Juliana's throat felt like glass
shattered inside it. Her head ached as she tried to sit
up, but she couldn't move. Heavy dry wool smothered
her face as if buried under a carpet of sharp pine
needles. She fought to get away from it and rolled on
the rocky ground into a body.

   Lukas pulled the hot, dry shawl to the side and
turned his head toward her. "See?" He scraped out. "We
lived."

   Sometime after she'd passed out, he must have
soaked her shawl and covered them.

   She tried a smile through dried, cracked lips. The
pull and sting stopped the attempt.

   He looked past her at the smoky sunshine spilling
through the entrance without raising his head off the

ground. He croaked through parched lips, "We lived."
Lukas touched his cracked lips dabbing at them with
the edge of the shawl.

She turned to follow his gaze. The blankets burned
off the posts, charred remains lay in tatters and ashes.
She squinted into the bright light grateful to see
another morning.

But Ed Pulaski lay nearest the exit. No sounds. Not
even the heavy breathing of the horses. Was anyone
alive besides them?

She sat up slowly, unable to hold back hacking
coughs at the still, smoky air.

Lukas did also, though coughing hard, he moved to
block her view of the horses. "Don't look." He put his
hand up and curved his palm around her cheek. "The
poor beasts are gone. Let's see if there's anyone we can
help."

Juliana's lips trembled, but she nodded.

A few others stirred until most were making their
way to the front. A long, painful walk for such a short
space.

Groggy, sick from the smoke inhalation, Lukas and
Juliana joined the others who could move under their
own power.

Lukas counted those that would never rise again.
"Five men down, and the two horses."

"Looks like Big Ed didn't make it either." One of the
firemen called back as he hunkered over Pulaski's still
body. "The boss is dead."

"No, he's not." Ed Pulaski pushed onto his elbows
with a heavy grunt. Most of his hair had been burned
off and blisters covered his eyes. But he lifted his chin

to savor the fresh air circulating through. "Might need some help getting home, boys."

A collective sigh sufficed as their cheer.

Shuffling up with a couple blankets, the strongest men created a makeshift stretcher between them. Those that could, helped Ed onto the blankets. With the plan to trade places as needed, the group set out toward home and help.

Lukas wrapped his arms around Juliana. "Let's get going, we have a wedding to get to. You do plan to keep your promise?"

Juliana raised on tiptoe, touched his sooty cheek, and in a scratchy voice said, "I do."

CHAPTER 14

"I NOW PRONOUNCE YOU MAN AND WIFE. YOU may kiss your bride." The preacher laughed with them over their torn, scraggly clothing. "Though I've never seen a couple in such condition. I'll be glad to look back on this day that something good came out of that big blowup."

Lukas gently rubbed his thumbs across his wife's scratched knuckles and then leaned in and barely touched his lips to Juliana's. Neither could take much more in their state.

As he raised his head, he said, "Sooty and scratched, you are the most beautiful bride in the world." He smoothed her tangled hair away from her bruised cheek.

She smiled into his eyes. "You got us safely out. I will follow you anywhere." Then she took a long look around what remained of Wallace, Idaho. "But where do we go from here?"

The preacher pointed to the coming train. "I hear

folks in Montana are welcoming survivors in Missoula and Helena. There's a lot going on over there for an industrious couple such as yourselves."

Juliana searched Lukas' face. "Do you suppose they'd like a baker and a teacher there? Or do you have to go back and rebuild?"

"That's up to you." Lukas answered.

The preacher took a step down from the altar. "I hear they're growing so fast they need all sorts." He patted Lukas on the shoulder. "Most folks need to make their own opportunities. You could make as much there as working for the mines, if you do it right. Sounds like you both have the skills."

"Opportunity, yes. This is why I came to America." He put an arm around Juliana. "This is what we'll do. Yes?"

"Yes." She whispered, rapture and relief washing over her adorably dirty face.

The preacher stretched out a hand. Lukas took it and they shook. "Might not be the best wedding supper, but the ladies of our church have good food ready. They've been feeding all the fire fighters and survivors since yesterday. You'll be a bright spot if you'll let them feed you before catching the train."

They followed the minister out of the red brick chapel and around the side toward the back.

Juliana's eyes misted. "What about your mother and sister? Everything is gone. How will you bring them now?"

Lucas stopped and hugged her. "They're already on the way."

"They are? How?"

"I sent tickets via the agent earlier in the week."

"You did?"

"I've always kept my accounts away from the camps. Too much desperation and too much risk. The company agent deposits my pay in the bank and has set aside funds for my family all summer."

"I did too, deposit with the agent, I mean."

"You did?" Lukas shook his head. "I thought you meant you'd lost all your money in the fire."

"No. I lost all my kitchen tools," her voice dropped into a husky tone. "And my keepsakes." She lifted a hand to his scruffy chin. "But I didn't lose you or our future."

"I'm sorry you lost all those things, though."

"Me, too." She touched two fingers to her temple. "Those memories are here…" She touched her heart. "And here forever. But I suppose the pastry shop will start out a little smaller than it would have. Maybe I'll be able to buy some used items."

Lukas kissed her light as a dew on a cobweb. "Oh my lovely wife…you haven't met my mother yet. She may very well have already packed everything you need."

"How in the world would she know?"

He shrugged. "She may have already heard about your dream."

"What do you mean?"

"I wrote to her, after I first looked into your eyes. I kept writing. She wrote back that she would sell all but her best utensils and bring them for you as a wedding gift. We may have lost our land, but the manor had an extensive kitchen."

"That was mighty bold of you." She plopped her hands on her waist. "What if I'd never agreed to marry you? You'd have had a trunk full of useless pots and pans."

"No. I would have done this—" He scooped her up to a flurry of giggles. He held her close as her arms tightened around his neck, and strode toward their waiting meal, carrying her over the threshold of the fellowship hall.

"I see, Mr. Filips, you would abscond with my heart?"

"Mrs. Filips, I already have." He kissed her before setting her on her feet to receive the good wishes of a room full of strangers. Strangers that shared the joy of a future and a hope amidst the smoking mountains.

MONTANA TRAVEL TIPS

Riding the Route of the Hiawatha is exhilarating, terrifying in the pitch black tunnel, dizzying peering over the trestles into streams hundreds of feet below, and rewarding as you ride to the finish line where the shuttle waits to deliver riders back to their cars.

The first, terrifying train tunnel is the darkest place I've ever encountered. And cold! When you start the ride from the parking lot on a hot summer day, you don't expect to be so cold.

Our family layers up for the day because that's such a long ride it's nearly impossible to tough it out in the dark, wet tunnel. Though we've also been caught in early summer rains on the trail. The weather changes more than it stays the same up there on the Continental Divide. Properly prepared riders know they'll be in a variety of layers all day.

If you're aware, and you are now, be sure to stop halfway through the mile and a half tunnel to admire the hidden historic marker that joined the two teams digging and blasting their way through a mountain to meet in the middle. I didn't find it until the third time through!

The gorgeous waterfalls start right after the 1.66-mile tunnel. That first one is a great photo opportunity even though it's not that tall. It is lovely. Then you'll see a few others with streams flowing under trestles that feel like you're in the stratosphere.

Train Trestles allow a gorgeous view of the top of the Rocky Mountains. The views are so beautiful they're hard to believe. Pull over and read the historic markers, and then take photos of the world around you. I felt so small standing on a mountain next to the clouds.

Towns that once were are memorialized throughout the valleys. Stories of the people and the incredible hardships are well worth the read. Admiration is too small to describe my feelings about these incredible adventurers. It's almost too incredible to believe!

Getting there isn't hard. Coming from Idaho on I-90, you'll take Exit 0, as in zero. From the Montana side, again on I-90, you'll take Exit 5. But do check the website first for reservations, updates, and information. You'll find the website easy to navigate and super helpful: https://www.ridethehiawatha.com/getting-to-the-hiawatha

Gear and necessities include the brightest head lamp you can find! The regular bike lights will not safely navigate the St. Paul Pass tunnel at the start of the ride. Besides, you'll want to have enough light to admire that middle point marker, right?

Bring a coat, gloves, bike helmet, intense high-powered head light, snacks, a backpack for all the gear you won't use after the tunnel, water bottles, a bike (whether yours or a rental), and a really good camera or phone with camera. Remember there's little to no cell service so be sure to tell people when you're starting and let your emergency contacts know when you're done so they won't worry.

Camping is rustic. We've taken our RV and dry camped off the road, loving our time in nature. There are several pull outs, but not a lot of them and no services. Perfect if you're looking to get away from it all. There are some regular sites and lodging within a reasonable distance. Check the area camping/lodging guide here: https://www.ridethehiawatha.com/area-camping. Main cities are only a few hours drive. Since the bike trail takes about half a day with lunch, you could easily just go for the day.

Saying goodbye to this leg of our journey in this Montana history and travel series. Join me in other books, on Genealogy Publishing Coach, and at the National Institute for Genealogical Studies.

It's been my honor and pleasure to be your travel guide. If you've enjoyed your time with me, please consider sharing these books with your friends. Please do tell me if you decide to visit the places and spaces I've told you about. I'd love to hear.

Thank you for sticking with me through all six books. I hope to see you in future books, too.

—Angela

DEAR READER,

I hope you enjoyed *Flame of the Rockies*, book 6 in the **Queen of the Rockies** series. I loved sharing little-known true Montana history about the largest fire in US history. Little-known history easily becomes lost history. By sharing stories like this, we won't let it or the amazing people be forgotten. We won't forget their challenges, amazing accomplishments, and those who earned the right to be our heroic examples.

I wrote six stories that tell some of the special events and what happens as Montana becomes a state in the **Queen of the Rockies Series.** All six are available in e-book, paperback, and large print editions. I wrote them to keep us remembering.

As an author, I love feedback. Candidly, you're the reason I continued to explore the history of Montana. So tell me what you liked or loved, what questions or thoughts this book brought to mind, or what made you laugh and cry. You can write to me on the contact page of my website. I do answer emails personally.

Visit me on the web at: AngelaBreidenbach.com or tune into one of my podcasts, like Genealogy Publishing Coach, also easily found on my site. I hope you'll enjoy reading the stories I write and listening to my shows and interviews.

Finally, please consider writing a review for this book. Reviews help books sell and keep writers writing. Would you kindly leave a review on your favorite site such as Bookbub, Goodreads, Litsy, KOBO, B&N, Amazon, or any other review site?

Your feedback is important to me and very appreciated! Reviews can be hard to come by these days. You, the reader, have the power now to make or break a book. I hope your review will help us preserve history by connecting with more readers.

Thank you so much for reading *Flame of the Rockies*, spending time with the people of Montana, and I hope you'll also enjoy the sample of *Gems of Wisdom: The Treasure of Experience* because preserving your story is important to me as well. Sometimes that takes facing the tough stuff we've been through in order to triumph. Triumph isn't about "winning". Triumph is taking those trials and helping others with what we've learned.

You'll find the *Gems of Wisdom* sample at the end of this section. I hope my story encourages you to tell yours. But most of all, I want to thank you for spending time with me. I'll see you in the pages of the next book.

If you'd like to receive new release information, genealogy tips, or keep up with me through my newsletter please consider signing up when you visit my website or you can join at this link:

https://landing.mailerlite.com/webforms/
landing/n0s2t2

Honored by your time,
Angela Breidenbach

Did you miss the beginning of Frankie and Joey's story in *Queen of the Rockies*?

What if you were caught doing something good, but the man you loved didn't see it that way? Meet Calista Blythe and Albert Shanahan in 1889...

Queen of the Rockies, **Book 1** and kick off title of the series by Angela Breidenbach ~ 1889 (Helena, MT): Calista Blythe enters the first Miss Snowflake Pageant celebrating Montana statehood to expose the plight of street urchins. But hiding an indentured orphan could unravel Calista's reputation, and her budding romance with pageant organizer, Albert Shanahan, if her secret is revealed. Will love or law prevail?

Song of the Rockies. 1890 Montana historical.

What would you do if you were given eleven rowdy street newsies and told either you turn them into model citizens or they get sold into indenture or sent to the military? *Song of the Rockies* is the story of a sweet music teacher, Mirielle Sheehan, and eleven boys given one chance or else! Evan Russell lost everything—his ranch, his wife, and now after trusting relatives with his young son, even the little boy is missing. How can a beautiful symphony of the heart come from such chaos? Reminiscent of Little Men.

Heart of the Rockies. 1892 Montana historical.

Could she believe in herself when no one else did?

A progressive thinker in 1892 Montana, Delphina O'Connor believed in God-given dreams for women didn't stop at marriage and children. Hers might not include a husband or family at all. So when Hugh Thomas rescues the new swimming instructor at the elegant Broadwater Natatorium from near drowning in the plunge, how can anyone believe the freedom to enjoy swimming, competition, and a healthy body is an appropriate activity for a proper lady? Hugh is about to find out status quo is the starting line for a courageous woman with a dream!

Heart of the Rockies explores the real-world question: What do you do when you think differently than the world around you?

Flower of the Rockies. 1892-1895 Montana historical.

Can you leave your past behind?

No one knows the real Emmalee Warren, or the sacrifices she's made for love. An infamous soiled dove of no consequence turned miner's widow. Men are coming out of the woodwork to stake their claim on her and the mine she inherited. They wanted her body before. Now they want her money, and they'll do anything to take it. But love and acceptance seem out of the question for Emmalee.

Society wants nothing to do with her regardless of her changed ways. Who can she turn to when her inheritance and chance at a future is at risk? Will she be forced back into the brothel to survive? Hiring a lawyer, Richard Lewis, to save her from financial ruin might let her start over somewhere else — if he can save a little of her finances from her husband's partner. She'll go anyplace else where no one knows Miss Ellie's name. Anywhere to leave the scorn behind. Becoming an unknown is the only way to freedom...or is it? Can she leave her past and build a new future?

Bride of the Rockies. 1893 Montana Historical

Would she give up her dream for love?

For botanist, Bettina Gilbert, mining is an offense against God's green earth. With the shortage of women in Montana, Luke travels to Chicago to manage the Montana mining exhibition hoping to also find a wife. Only that pretty botanist keeps disrupting his mining presentations ... and his chances of meeting the right woman! A city girl who despises his way of life would be the worst choice for a miner's wife, wouldn't she?

Flame of the Rockies. 1910 Montana Historical

August 1910, Idaho/Montana Border

Can she release her prejudice to love again? The fiery pain at her new husband's murder might equal the disaster blazing across the Pacific Northwest. Stranded in the treacherous railroad camp, baking bread for survival, Juliana Hayes has no desire to marry a railroad ruffian like Lukas Filips, or anyone else. Can she release her prejudice to love again? Or will either one of them survive The Big Blowup to find out?

Based on true history when three million acres burned out of control on the border of Montana and Idaho darkening the skies all the way to the East Coast. It's a wonder anyone survived!

BOOK CLUB QUESTIONS

1. How did life in 1910 compare to what you thought it was like before you read *Flame of the Rockies*?
2. How would you befriend someone whose pain or fear keeps them from connecting?
3. When is a good time to talk to someone who is grieving?
4. What goal are you determined to reach? Do you have a plan?
5. What if heroism meant living your life in pain like the true hero Edward Pulaski?
6. How much does a person's past matter?
7. People from many countries, spoke many languages, how do you find common ground?
8. One woman survived the Big Blowup by running 25 miles ahead of the fire. How did she do it?
9. Who was your favorite character in this story, and why?
10. What did you learn from the story, characters, or situations in Flame of the Rockies?

GEMS OF WISDOM:

THE TREASURE OF EXPERIENCE

Angela Breidenbach

GEMS OF WISDOM

THE TREASURE OF EXPERIENCE

A Grace Under Pressure Radio Book

About Gems of Wisdom: Discover how your past has prepared you for a beautiful future. A fascinating treasure hunt for unique gems of wisdom to turn past pain from emotional pirates and negative experiences into grace in tough situations, strength to overcome fear, and how to positively influence others.

Helping others is both uplifting and fulfilling. Live your best, most joyful when you put these confidence and relationship builders into your life.

Read the inspiring stories and experiences of women who've overcome difficult pasts, being victimized, and helplessness to become confident and courageous. Collect the beautiful Gems of Wisdom that God created for you.

Also available in large print edition, standard paperback, and ebook versions. Enjoy the sample of this popular women's study in this book. Get your copy and copies for your Bible study at AngelaBreidenbach.com

What Do People Say?

Angie has amazing passion and mission for helping others achieve their goals and live healthy, fulfilled lives. With her eye always on the Big Picture, she is an unending source of inspiration, energy and empowerment for others.

~ Tosca Lee – Author of Demon: A Memoir and Havah: Story of Eve.

. . .

Any cause Angie supports is truly blessed. She has so much energy and passion.
~ Linda Bauman – Owner, Market Place Media

It's the cover's fault—honest! I was hooked!
~Kathi Macias, author of No Greater Love, Extreme Devotion series and 30 books.

Angela presented a training program for my group. She was well prepared, inspiring and a lot of fun. I enjoyed the session, learned from her and highly recommend her to you.
~Marnie Swedberg (Leadership Mentor at Gifts of Encouragement, Inc.

Angie Breidenbach's book is thoughtful and insightful. This book offers encouragement in a heart-touching manner that leaves the reader blessed in the hope of God's faithfulness. Thank you, Angie for being brave enough to confront these battles head on, and for sharing your heart.
~Tracie Peterson, best-selling author

INTRODUCTION

FROM A PERSONAL PLACE: ANGIE'S STORY

Search for Wisdom as you would search for silver or hidden treasure. — Proverbs 2: 4, CEV

I ran before I fell apart. Door after door in the sterile clinic kept me out. Out in the hall. Out in public where privacy became the mythical siren song before I fell apart. I needed seclusion, and I needed it now — before I fell apart.

The final door swung open onto an empty treatment room that smelled of medicinal alcohol. The heavy door closed behind me, only to have a nurse catch it. I turned to beg for a moment, just one moment. But there'd be no moment. She entered wielding compassion.

I backed away from the sweetness of her weapon.

She advanced. And touched me.

I slid down the white paint and hit the cold tiles.

"Are you okay?" Her voice echoed from somewhere above me, tinny and distant.

Misery, at this moment, did not want company.

Eva, mother of two, my mom, was diagnosed with paranoid schizophrenia at twenty-three, around my second birthday. I never had that close mother-daughter relationship — and now I never would. I had to accept that no miracle medicine would give me the mother I'd craved my entire life.

I could not restore my mother's health or sanity. No doctor, no drug, nothing would make it all better. Nothing would change anything. Hope, the stuff of fairy tales, exploded. I reeled from the power.

Resigned, I rested my head against the wall. I could almost see the iridescent glitter of fine dust settle all around me. I closed my eyes.

What was left?

I still shiver when I think about that time, that emotional void. It was very dark down in that hole.

How was I supposed to see in the suffocating dark? Were valuable gems waiting to be discovered?

How dark is the place where you are right now? Have your hopes come face to face with reality? Are you lost in the dark looking for a way out? Let's strike a match and light the space right here.

I invite you on a treasure hunt, an adventure that reveals not only hidden treasures of experience, but also the pirates who try to steal it. An adventure that will give you tools to uncover the gems of wisdom that make this journey rewarding. This book is your trea-sure map. The stories and concepts in these pages will help you to delve inside and find your own gems of wisdom to fill up your treasure chest. The *Companion Guide* at the back of the book provides space to write your answers to the questions in the first part of the book. Helpful features include the following.

Pique Points: thought-provoking questions.

Ponder Points: tidbits to entice an open mind.

Personal Places: tender and true stories from the hearts of volunteers, shared to help others.

Pirates: creative fictional portrayals of cutthroat negative attitudes, situations, and feelings that get in the way of healthy living (based on real historical pirates because knowing history matters when we learn from it.)

Putting It All Together: tying all the loose ends together in each chapter so it's easy to understand and easy to put into practice.

Polishing Point: real-life options to solve real-life dilemmas and suggestions on how to put them into practice.

Gemstones: gems of wisdom awarded as new concepts learned along the treasure hunt route.

Definitions: a little more perspective on some words and ideas sprinkled throughout the book.

Tips: tried and true gem chips that have worked for others.

The *Gems of Wisdom Companion Guide* at the end of the book with space to record your answers to the questions included in each chapter.

Your captain and crew stand ready to help you navigate the changes ahead until you can pilot your own vessel. Come fill your treasure chest. Battle your pirates and win the gems of wisdom. You can win. You must win!

Ahoy there, matey. Welcome aboard!

CHAPTER 1 — WHAT'S FAIR?

Gemstone: Tanzanite

Pirate: Injustice

*Then I will purify them and put them to the test, just as gold
and silver are purified and tested. They will pray in my name,
and I will answer them. I will say, "You are my people," and they
will reply, "You, LORD, are our God!"*
— Zechariah 13:9, CEV

Heat treatment can turn ordinary gemstones into
extraordinary jewels. Tanzanite, straight from the
ground, is tinged brown. Dirt colored, plain old brown.
It's easy to take for granted as a valueless rock. But
heat that rock and watch the fire flare from the dazzle.
A kind of can't-take-your-eyes-off-it rich purple-blue
dazzle.

Tanzanite is most often cut into facets, adding more
dimensions to the jewel. The intensity comes from the
high temperature that purifies the color. Color that

makes you want to take a second look, draw in a little closer, and see it from every angle to absorb the beauty.

Record your answers to questions in the following sections in Chapter 1 of the *Companion Guide*.

Ponder Point

- How skewed is your fairness meter?

As a Christian, it seems as if I live in an open-air zoo. Passersby stop and stare. They watch my every move with fascination like a monkey in an exhibit. Sometimes the people on the other side of an invisible wall mock, taunt, and tease. Sometimes they throw words at me to get a reaction so they can tell their friends about the exciting visit to the zoo. But when a fellow monkey wants to fight over little things...

Safe in my little monkey enclosure, I don't need protection from my own kind. I don't expect to fight over the branch where I rest or the proper way to peel my banana. After all, we're compatible creatures, right?

When someone trustworthy attacks, it feels like a hairy arm swipes at my fruit and bare teeth screech an unbearable noise demanding to be in command. Other monkeys watch the commotion as my attacker bites and claws and leaves open sores to scar forever. She wasn't even hungry. She had a pile of bananas under her own branch.

I want to run and hide from the unnecessary malice. I plead for respite from my Zookeeper. I want to go to a safe enclosure away from the mean monkey. The Zookeeper holds me, binds my wounds, and gives me back my banana. But he doesn't take the bad monkey out. Instead, he approaches the offender with love. I watch, huddled with pouting, tearful eyes.

The Zookeeper opens his arms to the nasty, selfish monkey. She leaps into them, grasping and clinging, and drops a little bundle in the process. The tiny body is no longer breathing. He picks up and cradles the little lost one. Zookeeper pulls the mean monkey deeper into his embrace.

I needed holding.

"She attacked out of confusion and fear." He looks over to me. "Her heart is sick." It wasn't evident by the way she looked on the outside and the skill she used to keep the hurt hidden. "Oh, my gentle soul," he says. "It is not the healthy who need a doctor, but the sick. Come."

We are both sick and in need of our Zookeeper's care.

Pique Points

- Do people hide things they don't know how to deal with?
- Is being fair really the issue?
- How skewed is my fairness meter?

Personal Place: Rachel's Story

Rachel sat at the cramped kitchen table, waiting for the coffee to percolate. The light green wood stove crackled from behind, and the stone fireplace popped sap in the flames like sharp bubblegum snaps.

We'd just finished a late-night chat about losing our moms. Sadness settled like the quilt across the sofa. How awful the loss. How emotionally spent we were, up in the mountains, at that fall writer's retreat. We shared a closeness, a sisterhood, a recognition only found in knowing what the other had been through.

"You know what I hate?" she added as she looked me square in the eyes. "I hate it when people complain that they *have* to call their mother. I hate it when people complain that they *have* to go eat dinner with their mother on Sunday. I hate it when all they want to do is avoid their mom." She stared into the fire and watched a log slip off the wood grate as it burned apart.

"Yeah, I know what you mean." I sighed and turned back again to look at the same fire as it died.

"Like they don't appreciate their moms. I was really close to my mom. We talked all the time. How can someone not want to talk to their mom?"

I coughed, then swallowed. "I wish I could." I kept watching the fire disintegrate into ashes. Another sap pop ricocheted off the log-cabin walls.

"I guess I get really angry at people who still have their moms and don't understand what they have. It's not fair. It's not fair that they can go eat, talk and be with their mom, but don't want to. I want to and can't. That's not fair."

"Mmm." I glanced at her sideways and back at the flames.

"My best friend was killed homecoming night. I couldn't find a way out of my grief. My mom came to where I was curled on the couch. She pulled me to my feet. Mom marched me out to rent some movies and buy ice cream and candy bars. So we sugared out that night."

Rachel smiled with a shrug. "We cuddled back up on the couch with a big bowl of popcorn and the movie. She told me she'd be my best friend. And every weekend for the next year, wherever I went, she went. She acted like she was seventeen. For me, she acted like the friend I'd lost."

I smiled over at Rachel. At her poignancy over losing a mom who was a friend. I wondered what that would have been like — a connected mom. I couldn't begin to picture it. Way too foreign. Way too painful. I had dreamed of exactly that. Someone to ask about boys, relationships, having babies — you know, a mom who was interested and ate chocolate with me. A mom who could track a conversation would have been nice. I'd have settled for that kind of mom even without the chocolate.

"I just want to be able to talk with my mom the way I used to sometimes."

I wanted to talk to my mom, really talk to my mom — once — ever. I looked all around the cabin, everywhere except at Rachel.

"I miss her. She was my friend, my confidante, my champion, you know?" Rachel's eyes glistened. "She listened and was there when I needed her." She plunked her chin into one palm, elbow resting on the wooden table. "Ya know?"

I breathed in the scent of the log fire. "No," I tried not to sound, well, harsh as I thought of my mentally ill mother who was unable to be a mom. Certainly no one I would ever share my deepest worries, wonders, or wants with. She wouldn't have understood. Some nefarious F.B.I. agent was always trying to catch her. That's all she understood. Talk to her? Uh, no. Calm her and reassure her? Manage her? A much more ordinary occurrence. I cleared my throat. "But I wish I did."

Rachel zeroed in on me like a hunter on an elk through a gun sight. Her mouth formed a silent "O" as she locked eyes on her target. The fire shot off another round, and the room went silent.

"I guess it's all relative, isn't it?" I shrugged and turned away. The fire's death fascinated me. "This fairness thing – it's all relative."

Rachel agreed. "One person has a mom and doesn't realize how special she is. Another loved a special mom and lost her." Her voice lowered, "And then some people have a mom but never really have her at all — like you." As if someone wiser had blown through her spirit, the shimmering drops that clung to Rachel's lower lashes diminished. The lines on the bridge of her nose eased. "Maybe fairness isn't the issue. Maybe things just are the way they are."

"Mmm," I said again. "They are."

Pique Points

- Does it make you feel better to long for options, more money or — a mom?
- Is it worth being stuck in the cycle of injustice?
- When is it time to stop your unreasonable wish for the scale to tip in your favor?

Putting It All Together

A little girl hung out the car window with a massive rush of summer wind on her face. She laughed with her older brothers as they zipped down the road. Teasing, one dared her to spit into the wind. She did. To her shock, the spittle arced right back into her face.

She couldn't fight the wind. From then on, she used the wind's power at her back instead of fighting it head-on. It took the one humiliating act to teach her that powerful lesson forever.

Why does it take so much for us to learn the inevitable?

The parameter of reality helps us to see the decisions we can make rather than those we wish we could make.

Pirates

The old saying "There is honor among thieves" has some truth in it. A thief knows not to double-cross an accomplice, but he'll take *you* for everything. The golden age of piracy was a short time in history, maybe 1668–1722. A loose group formed called the Brethren of the Coast. They had their own code of ethics called Articles. For example, if a man stole from the "Company" then he would be marooned.

The Pirate of Injustice follows a set of rules, just not the same rules you think he should. Those rules determine a standard set of behaviors and beliefs. The problem is negative habits. Habits create a pattern of victimization that degrade into helplessness. Helplessness keeps us from taking charge of our lives and attaining the dreams that have been melded into our DNA by God.

It's amazing how these pirates tag team, isn't it? Worry about unfairness sets up ineffective, unproductive, and overwhelming feelings. Vision blurs. Tears fall. You can't fend off the waves of marauders. There's a lack of effort and purpose. The Pirate of Injustice laughs as he sees the sword and cannon going unused. It's much easier to attack a foundering ship with all the rusty weapons and the crew confused.

A good definition of injustice is "acts or conditions that cause people to suffer hardship or loss undeservedly."

Polishing Points

This is the moment to stop spitting into the wind. Stop allowing all that could be, or would be, to immobilize you.

Begin by jotting down your answers to the questions in Chapter 1 of the *Companion Guide*. Leaving issues unwritten allows the Pirate of Injustice easy access to your ship and your peace of mind. It's time to raise the sails and move out of Pirate's Cove with the wind at your back. Use a compass to plot your course, not a fairness meter.

In honor of your new resolve, claim the gemstone of wisdom on your treasure hunt by saying the following out loud.

Tanzanite represents the way things are. I will recognize that heat creates dazzling results. Today I am releasing my fairness meter. It doesn't work right anyway. This gem of wisdom belongs to me.

CHAPTER 2 — ACCEPTANCE

Gemstone: Moonstone
Pirates: Magical Thinking and Denial
When I was a child, I talked like a child, I thought like a child, I reasoned like a child. When I became a man, I put the ways of childhood behind me.
— 1st Corinthians 13: 11, NIV

The moonstone's glistening glow is an interesting quality called adularescence. When you move it around, the glow rolls with the stone. The right cut shows this special feature. But uncut, the iridescence of moonstone is unrecognizable. It takes an expert to know how to cut gemstones correctly.

The moonstone is usually set as a cabochon, polished instead of faceted, with an arched top. The arch appears to create moon-glow across the surface. Wear it, and you carry the light of the moon wherever you go. Ah, the romance of carrying moonbeams!

But for some, nighttime holds stress and anxiety.

What is beautiful and romantic to one person may be accepted with fateful resignation by another. Night will come. The moon will shine. But not for me. For me, it stretches shadows into monsters.

Record your answers to questions in the following sections in Chapter 2 of the *Companion Guide*.

Ponder Point

- How do you recognize when misperceptions skew reality?

Jason Jensen told us where to go. We'd chosen Jason rather than Amy. Jason seemed to be a little, well, brighter. He could tell us which road to take and how long we'd be on it. He could tell us before a turn was coming so we'd know to take it.

Amy, on the other hand, sometimes dropped off talking at exactly the moment we needed her directions. After the turn, she'd pop back in and mention we'd missed it. We deemed her blonde. It was easier than getting upset over it.

Our Japanese exchange student, still learning the English language, slept in the backseat. He vaguely listened to our chatter about how much better Jason Jensen was than Amy. He looked around the car through half-open eyes. He sat up and looked for a cell phone. Then he leaned forward and asked, "Who is this Jason you talk about? Where is he?"

"Right there," I pointed at the dashboard.

"There?"

"Yes, the GPS."

"What?" His questions tumbled over one another. "Why are you talking to him? Is there someone talking to you from someplace? Who is Amy?"

We started laughing. The conversation had made complete sense to my husband and me, bantering about our new toy's best setting. But to someone who still struggled with the language, it appeared that we were talking about a real person.

"Oh no, no. The voice choices on the GPS are named inside the little computer. One is a male named Jason. The other is a female voice named Amy." I smiled and pointed at the logo. "The brand of the GPS finder is Jensen. The male voice seems to be more accurate than the female voice. She has a glitch that drops words. So we call it Jason Jensen for fun."

"Oh, so why do you call it blonde?"

Stunned, my husband and I stared at each other. Didn't everyone know about blonde jokes? Blonde jokes take a lot of explaining to someone who has little personal experience with any blondes. In fact, he never did "get" the blonde jokes at all. They just seemed like discrimination to him. An eye-opener for two American brunettes!

Things were out of context for our Japanese exchange student awakened from a deep sleep. Yet he trusted us to drive him 1,000 miles to see a part of the world he'd never otherwise visit.

Acceptance is as much about the art of asking questions as it is realizing that you may not fully understand the answers. Go on the journey anyway. With the right directions, you'll end up at the planned destination. Celebrate arrival with pleasure and satisfaction.

It's impossible to know when an "Amy" might leave out an important tidbit or when the context is lost on someone new to the journey. Sometimes, you learn as you go. Trust the driver. Also, be willing to learn new things even if you are the driver!

Pique Points

- What seems a little out of context right now?
- Ask this: Am I fully awake and involved in the conversation?
- Does "normal" feel foreign?

Personal Place: Rachel's Story

The full sunlight burnished her auburn hair. It was long and near the shade of a burgundy maple deepening in the autumn. I marveled at the color difference in incandescent light, where it turned a mysterious shadowed sable. In candlelight, it shimmered with a vibrant satin sheen. That woman had the power to heal and the tangible, more powerful ability to love. And I — I was gifted with a part of her.

We once found a litter of kittens nearly frozen in a snow bank. Mama scooped up those tiny bodies, tucked them inside our jackets, and carried them home. They felt stiff and lifeless. Not a single movement. Not a single meow.

Mama lit the oven. She lit it so low that it became an incubator. All four of the little kitties went into a towel inside. She knelt beside the open door and waited. I knelt on the other side, watching. Her fingers massaged little backs and tested tips of minuscule ears.

Then it happened. One twitched. A gray and white tuft of hair on the tip of one ear twitched. Then a mewl, a very small meow.

I stared at the impossible. The aura of the ceiling light glowed around the edges of Mama's soft sable hair. This angel had a halo as four frozen felines came back to life by the touch from the magic healer, my mother. And I — I was gifted with a part of her.

One dark, rainy night, deep in winter, an uneven pounding on the door made me jump. After all, I was only ten. Mama answered to find a naked woman on the stoop. A bedraggled and bruised stark naked woman with long wet black, stringy hair. Her shaking body was covered in dirt and her fingernails gooped with mud.

Bloody lips whispered, "Please. Please."

As if she already knew a visitor was expected, Mama pulled a warmed blanket from a hook near the stove. She draped the blanket around from the front as she enveloped the tall, skinny woman in her love. Although not very large herself, my mother slid an arm behind the bleeding woman's back and another beneath her knees. Anyone would think she'd just plucked a child from the tub and cuddled her in a mother's embrace. She soothed a shocked woman-child with gentle words and her gingerly touch. She loved her. She loved everybody.

The next morning, I awoke to find a fresh-faced girl curled up on our sofa. I saw a black eye and a cut on her lower lip, but nothing of that horrendously beaten soul from the night before. Her hands had quit shaking, and she still didn't talk, but clean hair pulled into a ponytail and clothing from my mother's closet turned the girl into a completely different person — a healthy, whole person.

My mother smiled at me as she set a cup of coffee in front of our overnight guest. And I — I was gifted to be a part of her.

Then Mama grew ill – so ill. Her diabetes had gotten out of control. Two months after my high school graduation, she had her first heart attack. That was the realization for me that Mom was sick. I kind of always knew because she took medicine. I knew, but when she'd take it, she'd brush it off as "Oh, it's for my diabetes." Stunned at the heart attack, I knew a part of her was in the being of me. So I was there and held her hand. The healing part of her, in me, could work miracles.

Congestive heart failure set in. Every couple of months for five or six years, I'd fly to Oregon and stand at her bedside because she'd had a turn for the worse. I'd stand there, hold her hand, and she'd get better. This went on and on.

After I graduated from college, I moved to Oregon to take care of her. I had to go to a special class so that I could learn how to fill out the paperwork that said I was qualified to take care of my mother. I thought that was crap. A class to learn how to fill out paper? I was her daughter, and I still couldn't accept that she was sick. Even though she couldn't see and was missing toes. I couldn't accept it. But they were only toes.

I had to learn how to check her blood sugar. She taught me. She taught me about her disease. She was a nurse. She had to have peritoneal dialysis to act as a kidney. The solution was inserted into her abdomen through a special shunt that cleaned out her body. It had to be moved often, or her body would start to absorb it. Scary because she was running out of places for the shunt to be put into her scarred belly.

She would get better. She could draw on the strength and miracle of healing passed on to me and through me. And she would heal because I was gifted to be a part of her.

Taking those images from my childhood, where I felt like she could heal anything, I truly felt that all I needed to do was show up and wrap a blanket around her and hold her hand and she'd be better.

Until the end.

Mom was dropped out of the back of a transport and broke eight ribs, lacerated her liver, and punctured a lung. No one said anything. She was in such pain, but she didn't get an X-ray or follow up for several days. The fall had been omitted from her chart. The broken ribs and internal bleeding grew worse. Her little body became overrun with infection.

I wanted her to live. Why was she getting worse? She would heal because I wanted her to live. Up to the moment of her death, I wanted her to live.

That night Mom said, "Daddy, I miss you."

I'd been hanging on to her so much that she'd hung on here — for me. I did, I clung to her and wouldn't let her go. I still believed I could give my mother my strength. If I was with her, standing next to her hospital bed, I could give her my strength and she would get better. Seriously, I thought that. I did. Good grief! I really believed it. Because I was a part of her.

But when she spoke to her daddy, I couldn't hold her back any longer. I had to accept that I could not heal her. I had no magical powers. I only had the power of love. Love passed down to me through Mama. Love would let her go.

And I — I was gifted to be a part of her.

Pique Points

- Is childhood magical thinking somehow still an issue?
- Do you refuse to acknowledge the obvious because you deny reality?
- What time is being spent that holds you back from really productive living?
- How are loved ones held back from what they need?

Putting It All Together

Isn't it fun to play make-believe? Anyone can be anything. Any circumstance can come out how you plan it. Our imaginations and wishes on stars as the moon glows down on you blur the line between truth and fable. Until the sun sets, and you're left with the dark.

Growing up, your mind passes through that phase. You begin to understand and let go of mystical ideas. There's no man in the moon, no Jiminy Cricket, and no Santa and only the pretend belief in mermaids.

When life takes hard twists, sometimes we find that leftover pieces of childhood's imaginary ways become an obstacle. You cling to comfort, safe memories, and things that are known — as a child will often hide in a familiar place during a house fire rather than surrender to the firefighter's aid. Through the smoke, no one looks human. The masks, the axe and all the gear? From a little kid's viewpoint, the hero is a night terror come to life.

Denying the facts doesn't make our magical thinking any truer than hiding from shadow monsters in the moonlight. The more you believed it, the more your terror grew. The light of day revealed the clothes flung in the closet pile and off the back of the chair.

In the daylight, shapes are clearly visible. You can choose to hang the clothes and be rid of the scare. You can breathe and release the under-the-blanket-fear because of the new awareness that all around the room, coats are just coats and mounds of toys are not mountains hiding trolls.

Pirates

Ah, me maties, gather 'round as me friends here, the Pirates of Magical Thinking and Denial, are wantin' to steer ye off course.

Yo-ho-yo-ho, this tale is of the Siren's song.

She's a vision to a lad what's been at sea fer too long. And a beauty she is as she calls from the rocks. The Siren has long, soft hair spillin' down 'cross her bosom and a fish's tail curls up under her hips. But her song, it draws a man to her like rum calling an empty gut. Ye ain't heard nothin' like it! Many a strong gent's denied what's real for the sake of Siren's lies.

An inexperienced wayfarer can get mired in the melody. 'Tis easy on the ear and she's easy on the eye.

Siren's voice carries on the wind to tantalize a man's heartstrings. He wants that beautiful lass fer his own. To sing just fer him.

But take it from this old seadog, salty I am, she's a liar and a thief of men's souls. Oh, she promises to change her ways or offer safe passage. Ah, me boy-o, she never does.

Don't be gittin' caught in her spell. Not a bit of it. Her song'll turn yer heart ice cold the second she has you in her arms. Siren doesn't give back any opportunity for a life in her embrace. The sound is like a roarin' of a thousand seagulls at a fish market, ugly and squawking screams so high-pitched yer head'll near burst. Then she'll take you and dash you on the shoals.

Be ever on the ready if ye be hearin' the Siren's song. Turn away, boys, chart a different course. Never look her way or ye'll be lost to her magic.

Polishing Point

Another idea of acceptance is to be resigned *to* reality not *from* it.

Being resigned isn't quitting. That only counts in the job market. Resigned is more like a dawning that circumstances are what they are.

Some days dawn explodes when the sun leaps over the mountains, no clouds brave the brilliance. Some days it sneaks across a ridge, a snail's pace on a cold winter morning while clouds cloak the peaks. The dawn comes.

Acceptance is like the dawn. It will come. Certain times of the year, the moon is still visible while the sun is high in the sky. Almost as if it doesn't want to release the night all the way into the sun's care. "Hang on," it cries, "I'm not ready to leave."

Isn't that old wishes, old comforts, and expectations? Notice the key word: old.

It's time.

In chapter 2 of the Companion Guide, write down what would have happened, the dreams you had, and what you believed of the way perfect life should have been. Then write what you really see. What have other people noticed? Write the way it is now. Put it into words and escape the Siren's song. You don't need to be lost in the sea of magical thinking and broken on the rocks of denial.

Hint: They don't have to be pretty words at all. Not at all. Simply write a description of what is today's experience.

This is the beginning of acceptance. It is also the beginning of a journey and charting a new course. A journey carrying moonbeams instead of fearfully watching for shadow monsters.

As reality is revealed, prepare to feel long-buried emotions. Prepare to feel angry, cheated, and lost. You'll deal with those issues. For now, just be aware that you may feel them. Those feelings exist. Not anyone else's feelings, not anyone else's fault or responsibility. They just are.

Let's start a new theory: The moon shines for me, too, and I have choices.

In honor of your new resolves, claim the gemstone of wisdom on your treasure hunt by saying the following out loud.

This gem of wisdom, the moonstone, belongs to

me. The night is not too dark and shadows of magical thinking do not rule my adult world. I will practice recognizing the false securities of childhood beliefs and exchange them for the bright daylight, where I see clearly and can learn adult coping skills. I no longer fear loss, and I am not lost along the way.

Visit AngelaBreidenbach.com to get your copy of *Gems of Wisdom: The Treasure of Experience.*

ABOUT THE AUTHOR

Angela Breidenbach is a professional genealogist, media personality, bestselling author, and screenwriter. Angela lives in Montana with her hubby and Muse, a trained fe-lion, who shakes hands, rolls over, and jumps through a hoop. Surprisingly, Angela can also. Catch her show and podcast, *Genealogy Publishing Coach!*

Angela holds a number of certificates including in business management, coaching, lecturing, multimedia presentation, public speaking, methodology, English records, and more. She graduated from the National Institute for Genealogical Studies.

Affiliations include Christian Authors Network as president, Christian Independent Publishers Association, Alliance of Independent Authors, Faith-Hope-

Love Christian Writers, Daughters of the American Revolution—Bitter Root Chapter.

Social Media: @AngBreidenbach

AngelaBreidenbach.com
A-Muse-ings Newsletter: https://landing.mailerlite.com/webforms/landing/n0s2t2

BB bookbub.com/profile/angela-breidenbach
g goodreads.com/Angela_Breidenbach
P pinterest.com/angbreidenbach
twitter.com/AngBreidenbach
f facebook.com/AngBreidenbach
instagram.com/AngBreidenbach
a amazon.com/Angela-Breidenbach/e/B00460W4F4

LARGE PRINT EDITIONS BY
ANGELA BREIDENBACH

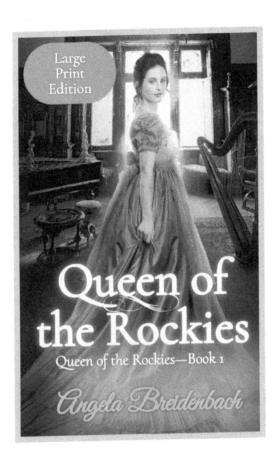

Queen of the Rockies Series comes in lovely large print editions as well as ebook and standard paperback.

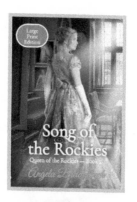

Song of the Rockies

Queen of the Rockies — Book 1

Angela Breidenbach

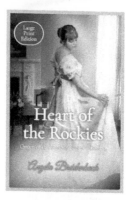

Heart of the Rockies

Queen of the Rockies — Book 3

Angela Breidenbach

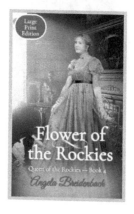

Flower of the Rockies

Queen of the Rockies — Book 4

Angela Breidenbach

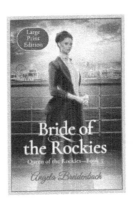

CPSIA information can be obtained
at www.ICGtesting.com
Printed in the USA
FSHW020117040222
88129FS

9 781957 132075